JAN   2023

TO

Also by Jen Calonita

12 TO 22

POV You Wake Up in the Future!

Jen Calonita

Delacorte Press

Text copyright © 2022 by Jen Calonita
Jacket art by Suzanne Lee. Background art (number balloons, gift box, and party items) © InkDrop/Alamy Stock Vector. Small pink gift box and envelope © Katsiaryna Hurava/Alamy Stock Photo. Photo of girl © Emil Pozar/Alamy Stock Photo

All rights reserved. Published in the United States by Delacorte Press, an imprint of Random House Children's Books, a division of Penguin Random House LLC, New York.

Delacorte Press is a registered trademark and the colophon is a trademark of Penguin Random House LLC.

Visit us on the Web! rhcbooks.com

Educators and librarians, for a variety of teaching tools, visit us at RHTeachersLibrarians.com

Library of Congress Cataloging-in-Publication Data is available upon request.
ISBN 978-0-593-43336-2 (hardcover) — ISBN 978-0-593-43338-6 (ebook)

The text of this book is set in 12.35-point Warnock Pro.
Interior design by Jen Valero

Printed in the United States of America
10 9 8 7 6 5 4 3 2 1
First Edition

For my goddaughter, Emma Neary.
Thanks for always sharing in the magic.

1

● ● ●

"I don't know about you, but I'm feeling twenty-twooooooo!"

It's a few minutes shy of seven a.m. and I'm belting out Taylor Swift at the top of my lungs.

Don't worry. I'm not waking anyone in this house. We've all been up since five, when my little sister, Reese the Wrecker, climbed out of her crib and turned on the TV in my parents' room at full volume.

"Twenty-two! Wa-hoo!" I sing louder, and hear a familiar growl come from my bed.

The small lump could easily be mistaken for a pillow. I pull back the covers and stare at the white Cavalier King Charles/Chihuahua puppy who is shooting me daggers with his soulful brown eyes.

"Morning, Milo," I say, scratching him behind his

long, floppy speckled brown ear. That stops his growling for a moment. "Is this too early for you?"

My best friend, Ava, spotted Milo at a shelter when she was volunteering there and knew I'd be obsessed with him. I've always loved Chihuahuas and Cavalier spaniels, but knew if I ever got a dog, it would have to be a rescue. There are just so many pets out there waiting for homes!

My parents weren't thrilled with the idea of letting me adopt Milo with a toddler in the house, but Ava helped me write a lengthy speech to persuade them. She's really good at speaking her mind, while I have a hard time even telling a server at the diner how I want my eggs cooked.

Ava's speech worked. I talked about how much I've always wanted a dog (fact!), and how responsible I am (I'm an epic big sister), *and* how I'd do all the dog walking, feeding, playing, etc., and they caved and said I could adopt him as a twelfth-birthday gift last November. Now they love him as much as I do and so does Reese, even if Milo is slightly terrified of her toddler tantrums.

"You know you love Taylor as much as I do, even at the crack of dawn." I start to sing again, and Milo starts to growl some more. I'm not sure why. Who doesn't want to hear me sing about how twenty-two is the age when I'll be happy, free, confused, and lonely all at the same time? Okay, maybe not confused and lonely, but I'll take the magical, freedom-filled part of being twenty-two in a heartbeat. It sounds incredible and looks it too, in Taylor's "22" video. In the video, she spends the whole time hanging with friends at the beach and then they go to a huge party. There's no math tests or homework when you're twenty-two. Just fun. The good news is at twelve and a half, I'm more than halfway there!

"Sing it with me, Milo!" I tell my puppy, who answers me by stretching, circling the blanket, and then burying his head under one of the pillows.

"Fine, be that way," I tell him, covering him back up so that he can sleep in total darkness. "Maybe I should have done a Billie Eilish song this morning. That would have fit your foul mood."

Billie songs are for days when I'm feeling angsty, like last Thursday, when I had to write an essay for English on *Call of the Wild*. I was so mad about what happens to Buck in the book I wrote an extra page and a half. But today I'm feeling fine, which is why it's a Taylor kind of morning. I turn back to my desk, where I've got my phone on a small stand and a ring light casting the perfect warm glow onto me and the mirror I'm staring into. I adjust the black hat I have on my head, make sure the camera can see my shirt—it says *NOT A LOT GOING ON AT THE MOMENT* (which is a shirt Taylor wears in the "22" video), yell to Alexa to start playing "22" again, and then press record on my phone.

I hum the music as I apply a thin layer of black mascara on my left eye. I've already applied a McIntosh-red lipstick similar to the one Taylor has on in the video, lined my eyes in black liner, and given them a wing tip. To finish the look, I pick up a pair of red heart-shaped sunglasses and put them on as I sing a few more lines; then I end the recording. I stand back, satisfied at the look I see in the mirror—classic Taylor.

"Standout lips, a dot of blush, and some eye-popping black liner," I tell Milo as I unclip my phone from the holder and watch the video, which I'll later sync to the actual Taylor song so you can't hear my bad vocals. (No one wants to hear *those*.) "I think I've nailed it. Maybe tomorrow I'll tackle the look Taylor has at the end of the video, when she's wearing the cat headband. I think Reese has one I can borrow."

Milo growls again.

"Don't worry. Reese isn't in here, and neither are any cats," I promise just as the door to my room bangs open and a toddler comes racing into the room. Looks like I spoke too soon.

"Harper UP!" demands Reese. She's wearing her favorite tee, with a dog on it that looks like Milo. I gave it to her for her second birthday. A juice stain covers the dog's ears on the shirt, and there's already something blue on Reese's pink pants. Nothing stays clean on this kid for long. Her green eyes lock on my phone, and her whole face lights up. "Harper? I SEE it?"

My phone is Reese's favorite thing in the world to hold. And drop. She's cracked the screen on my phone once already, and it hasn't worked exactly right since. No way I'm handing it over, kid. I quickly hide it behind my back. With my other hand, I push the makeup on my desk out of the way so that my sister can't get her hands on that either. I've still got a huge mascara stain streaked across my white desk from the last time she invaded my room.

"I see IT? PUL-EEZE? I SEE IT?" Her pudgy hands reach out to grab it. Suddenly, she stops and turns toward my bed. "ME-LOW? ME-LOW here?"

Uh-oh. She's on the hunt for Milo now too. Time for some evasive maneuvers. "Reese? Want to sing Tay Tay?"

My sister hears the magic words and stops babbling. Her voice lowers to a whisper. "Tay Tay?"

"Yes!" I take off my heart-shaped glasses and balance them on her nose. They're way too big for her face, which looks adorable.

While I always dreamed of having a sibling, I thought we'd be close in age so we could trade war stories about middle school and do each other's makeup like in Netflix movies, but Reese and I are almost ten years apart. My mom didn't think she could have children after me, and then, suddenly, nine years later, she had Reese. I adore her. She's cute—when she isn't being all Wreck-It Ralph and destroying things—but it's hard to have much in common with someone whose vocabulary consists of a few dozen words and whose favorite show is about talking dogs. But there is one thing we can both agree on: a love of Taylor.

"I don't know about you, but I'm feeling twenty-twoooo," I sing to her.

"Two!" Reese parrots.

"Twenty-two? What happened to twelve?" my dad asks as he appears in the doorway.

Reese sees him and squeals, throwing off the sunglasses and grabbing his legs. "No ME-LOW," she reports.

Dad ruffles her hair. "He's hiding, huh? I can't blame

him, or Harper for hanging in her room all morning to make videos." He gives me a pointed look.

I fix the pillows on my bed. "Hey, I like *Paw Patrol* and Cheerios as much as the next person, but if I have to get up early, I want to use my six a.m. hour wisely."

"Taylor today?" Dad points to my look, and I nod. "How'd your new video come out?"

"Good." I proudly pull my phone out of my back pocket to show him what I just shot. I keep the phone out of Reese's reach. ("I SEE IT?" she yells.)

"Wow, you look just like her, just with brown hair," Dad says, watching my clip.

"Don't I?" I hide my phone from Reese again. "I keep telling you TikTok is for more than dancing-baby videos."

"Uh-huh," says Dad, already distracted by Reese and moving out of the room.

Do it now, Harper, a little voice in my head says. Maybe it's Ava's since she's been coaching me to be more assertive. *Tell Mom and Dad why you're old enough to post on social media!* I race after Dad.

"You can learn a lot on there about cooking, travel, health tips, and pet care," I say, but I'm not sure he hears me. Reese is babbling away, the hair dryer is whirring in the next room, and Dad is looking busy. Is now the right time for me to try out the new speech I've been practicing with Ava? I think about what I want to say again: *I want to create content that teaches people how to re-create the makeup looks they see in videos in less time than it takes to sing the whole song. People post about makeup, but I want to show them how to actually get the look without having to spend a year's allowance, which is possible when you break down the looks step-by-step and use affordable beauty products.*

"What did you say, Harper?" Dad asks, turning to look at me as Reese tries to wriggle out of his arms.

Nope. Now is not the time. "Nothing." I twirl a strand of brown hair around my finger. I guess I'll save my TED Talk on "Why Harper Deserves to Post Online" for later.

"If it's about social media," Dad says, "you know the deal—you can watch all the videos on TikTok you want, but you can't post anything online or have followers on any platforms till you're thirteen."

I sigh. "I know." Never mind that Ana and Zach, my two best friends, have had accounts since they were ten. We'll also just forget that I'm pretty sure I'm the only seventh grader in Havervill, Massachusetts, who can't post on social media. Mom and Dad have this magic "thirteen" number in their head, and they won't budge.

My parents are forever giving speeches about how toxic social media can be for kids. I'm lucky they even let me have the usual apps (that was eleven-year-old me's battle). They don't want me zoning out and staring at videos all day, which I get. "Don't watch life—go live it," my mom is always saying. And I know she's right, but the minute the clock strikes twelve on my birthday in the fall, I'm going to make like Cinderella, start posting, and shout my username to the world. (Harperness13. Like "happiness" plus my age in six months.)

Only Six. More. Months. It's torture!

"Hey, just think of all the videos you'll have ready when you finally can post," Dad says as he swings Reese around and makes her laugh. "I know the world is going to love them. Pretty soon, you'll have more followers than that Blake girl you like so much."

A snort escapes my lips. "Blake Riley? Not possible."

"Why not?" Dad asks, sounding affronted. "You've got a good idea here. From what you've shown me, all that Blake girl does is talk about lip liner."

Blake is a beauty influencer on TikTok that I love. Her videos aren't produced or phony. They're just her in her room testing new beauty products that she breaks down by steals, values, and total splurges (I can never afford those items on my allowance). She's only twenty-two and is already one of TikTok's top earners. A year ago, no one had heard of her. She was a college cheerleader who was cut from the squad junior year. Bummed out that she couldn't dance and cheer for an audience anymore, she joined TikTok and started making beauty videos and now she's got over seventy million followers and has over four billion likes. *Billion!* She dropped out of college when all these major clothing and makeup brands started paying her to be an ambassador. Now she's living in some high-rise apartment in New York with other TikTok stars creating content, and she's starting her own affordable beauty line. I'm definitely going to buy everything she makes because she knows what she's talking about. Blake is so gorgeous it's depressing. She's flawless, like her makeup and hair. There's also talk of her starring in a new Netflix movie and maybe even launching a singing career. All because of TikTok.

Mom sticks her head out of the bathroom. "Honey, Blake Riley does way more than talk about lip liner." A curling iron is wound around a strand of her black hair, and her tan face is bare except for a swipe of blush on her cheeks. "She was just named the face of beauty for a skin care line and a major beauty company."

How and why does my mom know these things?

Because she works at UMass Lowell College, where she runs the school publicity department and handles their social media accounts. She knows a lot about social media (which is why she's so leery of me being on it). My dad works at the college as a history professor. They commute to work together and bring Reese to the campus day care.

"And she's done all that in less than a year online." Mom shakes her head. "There is no way that girl sleeps."

"NO sleep!" Reese says, starting to squirm out of Dad's arms at the thought of being put back in the crib. "No nap now! Nap later!"

"Not you, Ree," Dad says, kissing her nose and making her squeal.

People say Reese is my mini me—dark hair, freckles spreading across her nose and cheeks—but I don't see it. Our baby pictures are completely different. She has Mom's warm, tan complexion and these huge eyes and amazing lashes, while I do not. Plus, I was born with curly hair that has since straightened, while her hair is full of super-tight curls. She also has a bit of a temper, while Dad swears I was the easiest baby on the planet. Reese is anything but easy.

"By the time I'm allowed to post, people won't even

be using TikTok anymore," I lament. "I wish I were Blake Riley."

Mom grabs my chin and gives it a shake. "You are amazing just as you are, Harper Lancaster. Twelve and a half looks good on you."

I just smile. *If only I was thirteen . . . or twenty-two. Now, that age would look good on me!*

"Harper UP! Now Dadda? Now?" Reese tugs on his shirt.

"Yes, now." Dad looks at me. "Harper, we need you downstairs."

A small groan escapes my lips. "Do I really have to load the dishwasher before school? This shirt is white, and I really don't want to get anything on it."

Mom hands Reese off to me. "It's not the dishwasher. Reese has a surprise for you."

I look at Reese, squirming in my arms. "Up," she says solemnly.

"I'm already holding you, kid," I say, shifting my weight as I follow Dad down the stairs. She continues to babble on about ME-LOW and tries to find my phone ("I SEE IT?") while I try to remember if I have everything I need for the day already in my backpack—swimsuit, goggles, towel, swim cap for practice after school, that permission slip needed for the overnight field trip to Boston, and the math test I was supposed to do corrections on since I got a seventy-five on it. My heart sinks when I think of the test again. Math is not my strongest subject. Okay, it's my worst subject, and this year I'm really struggling in all my classes. Middle school is a lot harder than I thought it would be, and I can't wait for the school year to be over.

I'm so busy worrying about my math grade, I don't realize why Reese is screaming till we've entered the kitchen.

"UP!" Reese squeals, wriggling out of my arms and racing across the room to a wall of purple, pink, sparkly, and gray balloons that spread from floor to ceiling along with a stack of presents. I'm speechless.

"Happy half birthday, Harper!" Mom hands me an oversized cupcake with two inches of purple frosting on top.

"You remembered," I say in awe.

"Of course we remembered," Dad says, sounding indignant even while grinning.

"Not every day is your half birthday!" Mom agrees.

Half birthdays are a very big deal in our house. When my mom was a kid, my grandmother felt bad that her only daughter's birthday was the week after Christmas, when everyone was partied out and present-fatigued. That's why she started celebrating Mom's half birthday in the middle of the summer, when she could throw an epic party at the beach or pool and call on an ice cream truck to show up. Mom said when she had me right around Thanksgiving, she worried my birthday would be lost in the holiday shuffle, so she stuck with the tradition. November can be cold and dreary in Massachusetts, but half birthdays in May a few weeks before school gets out definitely liven things up. So do balloon walls.

"UP!" Reese cries with excitement, pointing to the balloons again.

"Ohhh," I realize. "She thinks the balloons are from the movie *Up*." It's one of Reese's favorites, which I find bizarre because it's so adult and sad. Give me *Tangled* any day.

"That's the real reason she got up at five a.m. today." Dad swoops in to keep Reese away from popping the balloon wall. "Last night I showed her the balloons after you retreated to your room for the night, and she couldn't wait for you to see it." He tickles her under her arm, and she giggles. "I didn't realize she'd try to spoil the surprise for you."

"She didn't. I'm completely surprised!" I say, taking my phone out to snap a picture of the wall to send to Ava and Zach. "I love it. Thank you." I hug each of them and kiss Reese on the nose.

"There's more," Mom says. "Presents! Want to open them fast before school?"

"Is TikTok used by over seven hundred and thirty-two million people monthly?" I ask.

Mom and Dad stare at me strangely.

"That means yes, obviously!" *Stop trying so hard, Harper.* I turn to my gifts, which are awesome. I get stationery from my favorite paper store. (I'm obsessed with note cards, pens, and notebooks with funny sayings on the covers like *THINGS I WAS RIGHT ABOUT.*) I also get a Sephora gift card, which I already know how I'll use, and I get two bright swim caps and new antifog goggles for swim team.

"There's one more," Mom says, holding up a small, glittery bag.

"You guys really went over the top for this half birthday," I say in awe.

"We just wanted to thank you for all the times you've watched Reese or helped out with her in the morning," Mom says.

"And at night or so we can go out to dinner," Dad adds.

"So this is basically babysitting back pay?" I tease.

"Bingo!" Dad says with a wink.

I see an opening and I take it. "You know, if you'd just okay me starting a dog-walking business with Ava, I'd make money of my own and wouldn't have to ask you guys for some whenever I go out after school."

"You're too young," Mom says automatically before I can attempt to form an argument.

Why is the answer to every question I ask "You're too young"?

"And Celia Darrow's mom agrees with me," Mom continues. "She won't let Celia babysit or get a job till she's at least fourteen."

"Fourteen? What happened to thirteen being the magic number?" I say, aghast. Sometimes I feel like with Reese around, all we talk about is potty training and kid shows and outlet safety precautions. It's as if Mom and Dad have forgotten I'm growing up. But I am. They can't pretend otherwise forever.

"Celia isn't haunting her mom about getting a job," Mom adds.

Celia doesn't have to, I want to say. *She already has a debit card and parents who are loaded.*

"We were just saying again, we don't know why you two don't hang out," Mom adds. "You have so much in common."

The only thing we have in common is that we're both in seventh grade at the same school. Celia is at the top of the food chain at Havervill, while my gym teacher still can't remember my name. I'm not even sure Celia does. But it's useless pointing this out to Mom. She and Celia's mom have been friends since—

"You two were best friends in preschool," Mom continues.

And she hasn't talked to me since, I want to say but don't as Mom is holding a present and I really want to know what's inside that bag.

Mom keeps going. "Speaking of which, would you like to—"

"Open!" Reese interrupts, and I've never been so thankful for a toddler in my life.

"Can I?" I ask, and Mom hands me the bag. But when I reach beyond the tissue, I find . . . nothing. "The bag is empty."

Mom grins excitedly and looks at Dad. "Check the bottom. There's a piece of paper."

I reach my hand in again and pull out the note written in Mom's loopy scrawl.

TikTok! What time is it? Insta Harper time!

"What does that mean?" I say with a snort. "Mom, this is the cheesiest thing you've ever written."

"Cheesy or not, it means you can post on social media!" Mom says, and my jaw almost hits the floor.

"You're joking, right?" I'm too stunned to scream.

Mom looks at Dad then back at me. "Nope! You've more than proven yourself around here with your sister and Milo—it's time we trusted you online too."

"And the videos you've been making are really creative," Dad adds. "You're right—it seems a shame that the only ones who get to watch them are us, Ava, Zach, and your grandmother."

I scream and toss the paper into the air, then lunge for Mom and Dad, enveloping them in a bear hug. "I am ready! I promise I won't get sucked in and be online ten hours a day!" Reese claps excitedly and yells, "Yeah!"

"You better not," Mom says sharply. "I really don't want you turning into a zombie who is just scrolling through mindless posts all day long."

"I won't," I swear.

"And we want to follow your accounts so we can monitor your followers," Dad says.

"You can," I promise. "I'll share all my TikToks with you when they're live. I wonder which one I should post first. Oooh! Maybe the one I did this morning about Taylor Swift's '22'?" I have finally joined the twenty-first century! "Thankyouthankyouthankyou!"

"You're welcome," Mom says, and holds out the cupcake again. She lights the candle on top. "Not to rush you, but morning traffic on 95 isn't pretty, so you need to make a wish."

I look at the candle and wonder: What should I wish for? I know it's not technically my birthday, but I've always made half-birthday wishes and sometimes they come true (I got my braces off two months early) and sometimes they don't (I'd really like to move up from this bralette into an actual bra).

"Make a wish! You must have one!" Dad encourages me. "Go ahead!"

I stare at the candle again and think hard about the right wish. Not to fail math? To be popular? To grow four inches? For Zach to like me as more than a friend? I wish . . . I wish . . .

Mom looks around. "Where is your phone? I'll take a picture of you blowing out the candle."

I look down at the table and frown. "It was just here."

Two seconds later, we hear a loud *POP!* and immediately turn to the balloon wall.

Reese.

She's got my phone in one hand and a plastic fork in her other. I see her eyes widen in surprise at the popped balloon lying at her feet. I take a deep breath. Sometimes if we don't react, she won't react, but this time, she starts to scream. Seconds later she hurls my phone across the room.

Mom and Dad rush over to Reese, half consoling, half admonishing her while I run for my phone. The case is cracked. I hold it up to show my parents.

"What do we say to Harper, Reese?" Mom asks.

"Sorry," comes her small voice.

My parents look at me.

Sorry doesn't always make things right, I want to say. But I don't. "It's okay."

I spy the cupcake still on the table. The flame has gone out.

Guess my half-birthday wish will have to wait.

In the car, on the way to school, with Reese watching *Peppa Pig* on the back-seat TV screen, I post my first-ever TikTok—the Taylor "22" beauty how-to, making sure to use some of the same hashtags I've seen Blake use in her posts. I send the post into the world and pray it winds up on For You pages. Then I text Ava and Zach.

> Parents have caved—I can post on TikTok! Go like my first post!

Zach

> WHAT????

Ava

> NO. WAY. I can't believe it.

Zach

We owe you a slushie!

Ava

Two slushies! I didn't think they'd let you before the magic 1-3.

Neither did I, but they did!

Ava

Next quest: Make them say yes to our dog-walking biz!

Trying!

Ava

Give them the speech I practiced with you!

They've got to stand still long enough for me to give the speech.

Ava

You're such a chicken.

22

I'm not.

Okay, yes I am.

Zach

H, this vid is really good! You look like a Swiftie.

Ava

Did you just compliment someone other than the Sox?

Zach

Don't start on the Sox! Or the Pats!

Not!

Ava

We don't care about either, Z. Only you do.

"So what do you say, Harper? Dinner tonight to celebrate the big half day?" Dad asks from the front passenger seat. "Besito?"

I look up from my phone at the word "besito." It's Ava's family's Mexican restaurant. I'm obsessed with their carne asada skillet tacos. The steak recipe is Ava's great-great-grandmother's. Her abuela runs the restaurant with Ava's parents. "Yes! Can I ask Zach and Ava? I mean, Ava might be there already doing homework, but—"

"But!" Reese repeats, breaking out of her TV daze to look at me. Then she sees my phone and throws the Peppa Pig stuffed animal in her arms. "Harper, I SEE it?"

"No way." I hand Peppa back to her.

"I think we should celebrate Harper's half birthday on Friday night," Mom says, not looking at me as she's driving. "And of course you can ask Zach and Ava to come too."

"Maybe Ava's abuela will make those sweet plantains I like as a dessert special," Dad says, looking wistful.

"Why can't we go tonight?" I ask.

"Because *you* already have plans—I meant to tell you earlier, but I forgot during presents. You've been invited to Celia's birthday dinner!"

My heart nearly stops. I yank on my right earlobe, almost pulling out one of my dangly beaded earrings

Ava made me. "I think I misheard you—did you say Celia?"

"Yes, Celia Darrow," Mom says. "Her mom called last night and said Celia wants you and Ava to join her at Sugar Crazy to celebrate."

"Me? And Ava?" I repeat. "Go to Celia's thirteenth birthday party?"

"Yes," Mom says with a laugh. "Why is this so hard to understand?"

Because she never talks to me, I want to say. "And it's at Sugar Crazy?" My voice has taken on a high-pitched sort of squeal.

Sugar Crazy is a dessert-themed restaurant with crazy shakes and drinks that smoke or light on fire and are topped with floating candy. They have hamburgers with multicolored rolls and crazy menu item names like "Harry Hamburgers Never Go Out of Styles." I've always wanted to go, but it's crazy expensive and almost impossible to get a reservation. My mom's friend from high school owns the place, and we still can't get in. I wonder how Celia pulled off having her birthday party there. "Why would she invite me? We don't hang out at all."

"It's middle school," Mom says. "Everyone is branching out. I'm sure Celia and her friends are too."

25

My heart starts to beat faster. Me have dinner with the Cambridge Street Girls? That's what Celia and her friends are called. The Cambridge Street Girls are a group of sixth, seventh, and eighth graders who all live on the same block. (Cambridge Street. Get it?) Their block is one of the nicest in town, filled with new-construction Victorians that are meant to look like old Victorians, and large lawns with in-ground pools and basketball hoops cemented in their driveways. Their families do everything together, even vacations. When I started at Havervill last year, I dreamed of moving to their block. I even started going on Zillow looking for houses for sale to show my parents, but no one moves off Cambridge Street. Why would they? The street address guarantees popularity, and Celia is the most popular girl in our school.

"So should I say yes?" Mom prods.

"Yes!" I say louder than I meant to. Middle school just got very exciting. "Does Ava know? She hasn't mentioned it." And I kind of think she would. She's not a big Celia fan.

"Celia's mom didn't have her mom's number, so I said you'd tell her." Mom pulls up to the curb across from school to let me out. "I'll let her know you are both coming."

"Okay!" My head is spinning. Celia invited me to her thirteenth birthday party! I don't know why, but middle school doors are clearly opening. I have a sudden vision of myself moving onto Cambridge Street and Celia and her friends welcoming me. *I wish, I wish, I wish.* I swing open the car door. I was already in a good mood this morning, but now I'm feeling epic. "Thanks for this morning! Bye, Reese the Wrecker!"

"Wrecker," Reese parrots, and waves goodbye.

With my phone firmly in my hand, I cross the street and head into school. I'm practically skipping until I reach the school's double doors. That's when reality sets in. I inhale as I step inside and I hear the shouting. I smell that musty two-day-old-lunch-in-someone's-locker scent and square my shoulders. It's like I'm preparing for battle. Another day in the trenches! Don't say anything stupid or mess up, or it will haunt you for the rest of the school year!

Havervill MS is just for sixth, seventh, and eighth graders. Our guidance counselors are constantly saying things like "This is a blip! You'll be in high school before you know it," but it doesn't feel that way when you're here every day. Sixth grade felt like the longest year ever. Everyone stared at you because you were the youngest. When you're in eighth grade, I have to assume everyone is staring at you because you're the oldest. Seventh grade is a safe zone in my opinion. No one bothers you. I've got a small group of friends who aren't always fighting (a plus from what I can tell with some of the drama going on in this place), but it's not like anyone is seeking us out either. Until now. I'm having dinner with Celia and the Cambridge Street Girls tonight!

Halfway down the crowded hallway, I see a bunch of brightly colored balloons floating above our row of lockers and know immediately they must be for Celia. Decorating lockers for birthdays is a must in this school. So is seeing neon wrapping paper with birthday cards covering the length of a locker. Sometimes there is also confetti, but the mess makes the custodians mad, so Principal Pearson made an announcement that all decorations must be contained to the locker itself. I don't see any confetti today, but I do see my two best friends, Ava Peña and Zach Kaur, waiting for me as I approach my locker, which is a few feet away from Celia's. That's when I realize the balloons are actually for me.

"Happy half birthday!" Ava shouts. She's so loud people in the hallway turn to look at the streamers, balloons, and sparkly red paper dotting my locker.

Attention doesn't bother Ava. She's the first to sign up to debate in class, is the student council treasurer, and has even shot a commercial for the shelter she volunteers at talking about rescue pets. But me? Attention makes my face burn. But could also be because Zach is handing me a small purple bag.

"For you, half-birthday girl!" Zach says. "And yes, my mom wrapped your present."

"Thanks," I murmur, trying extra hard not to look at his eyes, which are the most surreal shade of gray with flecks of green in them. Or at his blue polo that I once said looked good on him. Is he wearing it for me? Suddenly the hallway feels very warm and I have to reach out and hold on to my locker to stay steady.

Lately, I've started noticing things about Zach that I never have before. For example, I can't stop staring at this faint red mark he has above his right eye that he calls his "Anakin Skywalker scar." He got it watching a Sox game that went into extra innings. When they won, he accidentally tripped and crashed into a floor lamp. Another thing I've noticed: He loves Takis, is obsessed with all their flavors, and always has a bag with his lunch. He also knows the stat of every player in Major League Baseball and is an obsessive Sox fan who dreams of working for the team someday. I said working—not playing. Zach doesn't play sports, but he does love numbers and really wants a job in baseball analytics (which is basically the art of studying baseball stats and helping teams figure out the best players for their money—apparently it's all explained in this movie *Moneyball* that Zach is always begging us to watch with him).

So yes, I suddenly have a crush on one of my best friends. But no, I will never tell him. We are *friends*. Best friends. The three of us—Zach, me, and Ava— which means things would get really weird if two of us were dating. Ava has even said as much when I once wondered aloud about what kind of boyfriend Zach would be. ("Eww, no," Ava said. "And don't you think about it either. It would ruin everything.") And she's right. I know she's right, but . . . *Zach's eyes.* They're currently staring into mine.

"We were going to get you more notebooks and pens, but you already have a zillion of those," he says.

"I love it." I clutch the gift to my chest.

"You didn't even open it yet." Ava arches one of her perfectly full eyebrows.

"It's from you two, so I already know I'll love it." Inside the bag, I find a jade beaded bracelet with a silver charm hanging from it. The charm has an etching of Milo in it.

"Look on the back," Ava tells me.

I flip over the charm and see all three of our initials etched into it with the phrase "BFFs." "I love it!" I give them both hugs. "You guys didn't have to do all this." I stare at my locker, where they've each written me birthday messages and taped pictures of the three of us along with one of me with Milo, which is my favorite picture ever because Zach took it.

"How often do you turn twelve and a half and finally get to post online?" A strand of Zach's dark brown hair falls in front of his eyes. I resist the urge to brush the hair away. Seriously, the boy gives off an aura.

"Twelve and a half is turning out to be way better than plain twelve already," I tell them and look at Ava. "Guess where we're going to eat tonight?"

"If you say Besito, I'm already there most nights anyway." Ava hikes her books higher in her arms, giving me a view of all the animal stickers she's put on her binder.

I inhale before spilling the beans. I'm not sure if Ava is going to be excited or mad. "We've been invited to Celia's birthday party."

Ava blinks. "We what?"

"We're invited to Celia Darrow's birthday dinner at Sugar Crazy," I say, unable to hide my excitement.

"Whoa, you two are moving up the food chain," Zach says, leaning against my locker. "How did that happen?"

"Celia asked her mom to ask my mom to tell us to come tonight." I bounce up and down on my toes. I wonder if I'll run into Celia in the halls today. If I do, should I say something like "Thanks for inviting us"? Or is that dorky?

Ava's brow furrows and my eyes lock on one of her notebook stickers, which says "Pets Have Rights Too!" "That makes no sense. If Celia wanted us to go, why wouldn't she just ask us herself?"

"Because she doesn't have our numbers," I guess. "And it's Sugar Crazy. I'm sure she couldn't invite the world because it's so hard to get into and she didn't want others to feel bad." I look at Zach. "Sorry."

He holds his hands up. "I'm fine. I'm just going to live through your dining experience. I've been dying to try one of their twenty-dollar tie-dyed burgers."

"The buns are tie-dyed artificially," Ava says, sounding mad. "And they taste like paper."

"How do you know? Have you eaten there before?" I argue.

"No, but I know my abuela makes food that isn't crazy overpriced." Ava folds her arms across her chest and looks away.

"You're right," I try. "The food isn't going to be as good as Besito, but it's still going to be fun hanging out with new people. Don't you think?"

"She doesn't even talk to us." Ava can't let this go.

I bite my lower lip. "We said hey in the hallway yesterday on our way to Spanish."

"That's not talking," Ava argues. "You know I'm right! We're not Cambridge Street Girls. We don't want to be one of those posers anyway."

"Is it your birthday too?"

Ava and I spin around and pause.

The Cambridge Street Girls' unofficial leader, Celia Darrow, is standing in front of her locker staring at me.

3

● ● ●

Wait a minute.

Celia Darrow is talking to me? ME?

I think so, because she and her whole group of friends are staring at me and that has never happened before. I notice every girl she's with must have gotten the memo this morning—they're all wearing jeans with crop tops. My mom won't even buy me a crop top ("They're not appropriate for school"), but apparently Celia's mom doesn't feel the same way.

I notice she has several balloons hanging from her locker as well, along with dozens of sticky notes and pictures taped to her bright green locker door. She's holding two balloon numbers—1 and 3—in her right hand. She's thirteen today. Lucky.

"It's my half birthday," I say, the words escaping my lips before I can think them through. Did Celia hear what Ava said? I hope not. She doesn't look annoyed, so maybe all the pre-school noise in the hallway drowned her out.

"Half birthday?" Celia cocks her head, her strawberry-blond curls falling to one side. "I've never heard of anyone celebrating that before."

"It's this thing my family does," I say with a shrug. "Happy birthday, by the way." Do I mention dinner? She hasn't mentioned dinner. Maybe not everyone is invited?

"Thanks." Celia beams, her brown eyes lighting up. "So . . . do you get presents on your half birthday?"

"Yeah. My parents got me a Sephora gift card."

"I got one too," Celia says. "Is that store not the best?"

"The best," I agree. I look awkwardly at Ava and Zach. Celia hasn't acknowledged them yet. "I'm spending all my money on Benefit products," I add.

"Me too!" Celia says. "Their mascara is to die for."

"If you like theirs, you have to try Tarte's," I add. "They've got some great ones too."

Celia nods. "Noted."

Okay, what is happening here?

The Cambridge Street Girls stand behind Celia watching our exchange. Zach and Ava do the same. We've shared a locker near each other for a year and a half now and have never said more than "Hey, you

35

dropped your pen" to one another. Now we're bonding over a makeup store? Who knew beauty products could bring people together?

"Harper just posted a TikTok on how to copy Taylor Swift's look in one of her videos," Zach says out of nowhere, and we all turn to look at him. "She's Harperness13. It's her first post. You should follow her."

I know Zach means well, but I have a sudden urge to dive into my locker and stay there for the rest of the day.

"It's your first post?" says Celia's friend Saya, running a hand through her long black hair. All I know about her is that she's the best player on our middle school girls' lacrosse team.

"I just like to scroll," I say lamely, my face burning as they all stare at me. "But I figured it was about time I finally posted something." That sounds bad. *I think*. But Celia just nods.

"Gotcha," she says, running a hand through her hair. "I'll have to follow you."

"Really?" I sound too eager. I must sound less eager! "Okay. Cool. I'll follow you too." *Even though I'm already following you.*

"Blake Riley liked Celia's last post," Saya says. She's like Celia's spokesperson, always parroting everything she says and does and acting as her mouthpiece.

"Really?" I can't help sounding impressed.

Celia shrugs. "I did a Stitch video with one of hers, and I guess she liked it. It was nothing."

It isn't nothing. Celia has almost a thousand followers. Not five like me.

"Hey," Celia says suddenly. "Nice phone case." She holds up her own phone, and I notice she has the same glittery silver case that I do. Difference is hers doesn't have a huge crack in the back. "What happened to yours?"

I grimace. "My little sister threw it."

Celia swipes a perfectly curled strand of hair away from her eyes. "Call the company and say you bought it already broken. They'll have to send you another one."

"But it wasn't broken," Ava speaks up, even though Celia still hasn't acknowledged her. "She just told you her sister dropped it."

Celia rolls her eyes. "They don't know that." She looks at me again. "Trust me. It's fine. I do this sort of thing all the time."

Ava doesn't say anything, but I can tell from the look on her face she doesn't approve. I feel weird about it as well, but I'm not about to tell Celia that. "Great idea," I say instead.

"Well, I'll see you later," Celia says, and I notice

her typing something into her phone as she turns and walks away.

"See you later!" I call out. Later—as in her birthday dinner! I smile triumphantly at Ava as if to say, *See? It's not so crazy she invited us.*

I hear a ping on my phone and look down. NO. WAY. I hold up the screen to show Zach and Ava. "Look! Celia followed me on TikTok!"

Ava rolls her eyes. "She's too much, and her friends are such clones."

"Such clones," Zach agrees.

"But we're still going to her party, right? I told my mom I'd go, and I don't want to go alone." I make a begging motion with my hands and silently plead with Ava.

Ava groans. "If it means that much to you. We are not going to have fun. I know it."

"You're probably right," I say as I grab my books from my locker, but inwardly I can't help wondering what it would be like to be a Cambridge Street Girl. Even just for one day.

"See you at lunch," Ava says, and heads to the left.

"See you at lunch!" Zach and I call back, and we both head to the right.

And that is why first and second periods are my

favorite of the day (even if first is math). I get to walk with Zach.

"Ready for class?" Zach asks as we navigate our way down the hall.

"I'm never ready for math class," I say.

Zach steps to the side to let me slide around a large group of people blocking the hallway first (he's such a gentleman). "My offer still stands, you know—we can study for the next test together."

It's a great offer, but I'm also not sure how much I'd learn if it was just me and Zach sitting alone at his kitchen table. I doubt I could concentrate. "I may take you up on that," I say, pushing the invitation off again. I can see the math room up ahead, and instantly my stomach fills with dread. "I do not want to go in there."

"Then don't," Zach surprises me by saying. He's usually the first one in the room. Unlike me, he's good at math. "We still have three minutes, and the first bell hasn't even rung." He smiles. "Which means I still have time to give you your real half-birthday gift. Well, part of it." He takes my arm and pulls me out of the throngs of people and into the stairwell. People are streaming up and down the stairs, but no one seems to care that the two of us are standing off to the side, Zach rummaging around in his beat-up olive-green backpack, which is covered with patches from all the national parks where he and his dad have gone hiking. (Still on his most-wanted list: Grand Teton National Park in Wyoming.)

"But you already gave me my present," I remind him as he continues to hunt in his bag for another gift.

"That was from me and Ava," he says to the bag, not looking my way. "This is just from me."

Just from me. My heart starts to beat fast. Zach has never bought me a solo gift before. The three of us always team up on presents, with two buying the birthday person a gift together. If Zach is buying me something on his own, that must mean something. Right?

"You didn't have to do that," I say, suddenly very aware that the two of us are standing in a major inter-section of school.

"I know I didn't have to. I wanted to, because— Found it!" He pulls a wad of green tissue paper out of his bag and thrusts it at me.

Because why? I want to shout. I look down at my trembling hands in surprise. Whatever is in this tissue paper is the size of a book.

"Open it!" Zach says with a smile.

I peel back the paper and find two things nestled inside—one is an oversized pair of black sunglasses.

Below it is a beautiful white silk scarf printed with pinks and gold that looks very familiar. I pull them both out and stare at Zach incredulously. "This looks just like the one Olivia Rodrigo wore in the 'Déjà Vu' video!"

Zach nods. "I know you've been looking everywhere for one just like it so you can do a makeup video. Can't be Olivia without the scarf."

I spy the designer tag and feel ill. I know how much this scarf cost. He's heard me talk about trying to find a knockoff just like Olivia's for months. I swore to my parents I'd wear the scarf every time I was in a convertible cruising around Malibu, but since we live in Massachusetts, they weren't really swayed. "I can't take this. You spent too much."

"My snow shoveling business last winter was huge," Zach reminds me. "I've had this scarf put aside for you for months."

My stomach feels like it might bottom out. "You have?" I ask as the first morning bell rings. We have to get moving. We head to the stairs, me still cradling the scarf and the glasses in the tissue paper. "But still— it's just my half birthday. And you already got me the bracelet with Ava. This is too much."

Zach places a hand on my arm as we climb the stairs. "You, Harper Lancaster, are worth it."

4

• • •

You, Harper Lancaster, are worth it. Zach's words ring in my head all day at school and through an hour of laps at swim practice. They're pretty much all I can and do think about till I turn my phone back on after practice. My phone instantly lights up with texts. I see Grandma's name on the list and open her text first.

GMA

Your Taylor video is on my FYP!

Yes, my grandma has a TikTok account, and believe it or not, she has thousands of followers thanks to her videos. They're all posts of herself reading to her Great Dane, Mimi, and apparently people flip for grandmas-reading-to-dogs videos. Something tells me Grandma is the one who convinced Mom and Dad to let me online early.

> GMA!!! THX!!!!

GMA

It already has three hundred and forty-two likes and almost a thousand views! Nice job, kiddo!

What? That can't be right, can it? I open TikTok and look at my profile page, and *whoa*. Grandma's right! I've somehow gained four hundred followers!

> How did this happen?

GMA

The power of Taylor! You're going to be huge! I can feel it.

I love Grandma. She gets me and treats me like an adult. She agrees that between how responsible I am with Reese and Milo, helping out around the house, and doing swim team, I'm more than ready to have my own dog-walking business with Ava. But no matter how often she tries to talk to Mom and Dad on my behalf, they're still super strict with the no-job-you're-too-young-to-even-go-alone-to-the-mall stuff. Today was a big breakthrough with letting me post on social media, but I don't understand why my parents won't let me grow up. Why am I old enough to watch a two-year-old but not old enough to be dropped off at the movies with Ava and Zach?

I think again about the half-birthday-candle wish I didn't get to make this a.m. If Reese hadn't interrupted the moment, and I'd made a wish, I now know what I'd ask for: to be treated like a grown-up.

But tonight's birthday wish isn't mine. It's Celia's, and I need to turn my attention to her party. Being invited is a big deal and I've got a thousand and one questions. What do I wear? What will Celia and her friends be wearing? What do I talk about (TikTok is a must) and not talk about (Reese the Wrecker)? Who will I be seated next to at dinner? Ava, for sure, but who will be seated on the other side of me? Will we get along? Will we have anything to say to each other? And how do I get Celia's attention again? If she invited me, she must want to talk to me. Right?

My phone pings.

Zach

> Are you checking out your TikTok numbers?

Zach

> This keeps up, you could have a few thousand likes by midnight.

I open the app again, see my numbers for myself, and let out a little squeal that makes Milo come running. My post is up to seven hundred likes and three thousand views! People like my video!

> I can't believe it.
> Maybe it's a glitch. LOL

Zach

> It's not a glitch! You're killing it!

> Should I post a second video?

> No. See what this one does. Then you can try one with one of those new TikTok filters. There's even a birthday one.

A birthday filter? I wonder what that is. Zach knows numbers, so I believe him about the post continuing to climb. Plus, it's Zach. I'd believe him no matter what he said. I pause. Should I bring up my bonus half-birthday gift?

How can I not?

> Thx again BTW. Love the scarf and glasses!

Zach

> Good. Hope this is the best half bday ever. 🖤

And he signs the text with a heart emoji! A PINK HEART! It's not a red one, but it has to mean something. I hesitate—do I text a heart back? My heart beats faster. No. No. That's too much, but what does a heart emoji mean? I need to know! Who can I ask? Not Mom. Grandma won't know, I'm sure, and I don't think I can talk to Ava about this, but she's the one I want to talk to. Maybe I can find a way.

> Hey! You there? What are you wearing tonight?

I see three dots appear then disappear then appear again. Then nothing. Okay, she's still in a foul mood about having to go to Celia's. I cannot ask her about Zach. But nothing can kill my good mood. A bonus half-birthday gift and a heart emoji from Zach! I crank up the Taylor music and take a deep dive on TikTok, looking at Celia's videos trying to figure out what I should wear to the party. Some are stop-motion, others are her lip-synching, but the one thing all have in common is a few hundred likes. It makes me wonder how she got Blake Riley to like her video. I click over to watch Blake's latest post and see she's at some epic beach-front pool somewhere splashing around with a group of friends talking about some new energy drink she's now the ambassador for. Even Blake's pool look is perfect. Her hair falls in long, perfect ringlets as she sings some song I don't recognize while she twirls around on a pink doughnut float. Her two-piece bathing suit shows off her taut, tanned waist. I am not tan. I am not taut. My parents don't believe in two-pieces. And I don't have curves like she does either. Who knows if I ever will? I sigh and throw myself onto my bed, making Milo jump. I feel stuck in limbo between being the kid my parents want me to be and the adult I long to be. I just want to be twenty-two like Blake already!

My phone buzzes again. And I can't believe the time. How long was I scrolling, anyway? I look at the text. It's from Ava.

Ava

My mom will pick you up in thirty.
Show your parents this before I get
there. It's our dog-walking logo!

I stare at the image she's sent and can't help being impressed. While I was busy scrolling TikTok, Ava made a logo for our business. She's drawn a silhouette of two girls walking a big and small dog together with the words "Walk with H&A" under it. There is even a tagline: "Have your dog walked by the best! Responsible middle schoolers with affordable pricing!"

Is there anything Ava isn't good at? Her grades are through the roof, while I coast by with mid-eighties on everything. She's got the fastest backstroke time on the swim team, and she is racking up community service hours for fun by volunteering every Saturday at Muddy Paws pet rescue shelter. I wanted to volunteer too, but my parents said they didn't think they could commit to getting me there every week when they have so much going on with Reese. I secretly think it goes back to them not wanting me to have a job yet—even a volunteer one—but anytime I try to bring up how great it would be for me, I choke. I don't know how to have this conversation. Whenever I'm put on the spot—in class, with my parents, with people like Celia who are cooler than me—I just forget how to speak. I get anxious saying what is really on my mind.

Ava

So??? Do you like the logo???

Love it!

Ava

Show your parents! Talk to them!

I'll try . . .

Ava

You can do this. Just tell them why this job will be so great. TALK TO THEM.

Okay!

You mean now? Before Celia's?

Ava

Yes now!

Ava

And we have to still go to Celia's, right?

The text is followed by a sad-face emoji. I know she really doesn't want to go to this party, but I do. If Ava doesn't want to hang with Celia again after this one dinner, then fine, but it would be rude to dis someone on their birthday. I try to sound upbeat over text.

> It's going to be fun. See you soon! And wish me luck with my parents!

Ava sends me a fingers-crossed emoji, but I'm going to need more than an emoji to get through to them. Blake Riley's parents let her drop out of college to pursue her dreams of being a TikTok star! All I'm asking is to be able to walk someone's golden retriever on a Saturday morning. I am rehearsing what I want to say to my parents in my head when I hear an earsplitting scream downstairs.

Reese.

"Harper!" Mom yells from the bathroom. "Go see what your sister is doing! I'll be right there!"

I'm out my door in seconds with Milo jumping off my bed and on my heels. Down the steps I go, where I find Reese in the living room throwing wood blocks. One narrowly misses clocking Milo. I grab Reese and pick her up.

"Hey. Not nice," I say. "You almost hit Milo."

Reese blinks. "ME-LOW?"

"Yes. Milo. You could have hurt him."

She rubs her eyes and yawns. I look at the clock in the kitchen. It's seven p.m., her bedtime. She's tired. That gives me an idea. If I put her to bed for Mom and Dad, then I'll have a few minutes to talk to them before Ava gets here.

"Come on. Let's get you to bed," I say, carrying her to the stairs.

"No nap now! Nap later!" she says, starting to squirm.

I talk in quiet tones. "Harper is going to bed. Milo too. Come on, Milo!" I call, and Milo, thankfully, knows the drill. He trots along next to me. I click off the TV. "Good night, Peppa!"

Reese looks from me to the TV skeptically. "Night, Peppa."

"Sleep well!" I sing and head up the stairs. "Want to help me put Milo to sleep?"

Reese looks down at the dog, giving him the side-eye. "ME-LOW sleep?"

At two and a half, she might be on to me, but I keep going. "Yep!" We walk into my room, and Milo wags his tail. I put Reese down next to him and hand her his favorite blanket. It's my fuzzy Marvel superhero one that Milo has claimed is his own. "Tuck him in." Milo jumps into the bed when he sees the blanket, and Reese drops it on top of him. "Say night, Milo!"

"Nap, ME-LOW!" Reese pats the blanket and giggles. Milo, thankfully, stays under there till Reese toddles away. I grab her and carry her into her room.

"Harper is going to nap too," I say, and fake yawn.

"Nap too," Reese says quietly, her voice getting softer. "Nap now?"

"Yes, nap now," I say, dropping her into the crib. It's only then that I notice she's got something tightly closed in her fist. "What's that?" I try to pry it out of her fingers, and she tightens her grip for a second before she sees her Peppa stuffed animal and drops it.

It's my bracelet from Ava and Zach. How did she even get this? It's in one piece, but I'm still annoyed. Reese is constantly taking my things. When I'm twenty-two, I'm going to have my own place and no one is going to touch my stuff unless they ask permission first. (You know, in case I have roommates and can't afford my own place in Boston. I want to live in a huge high-rise with a doorman, and I suspect they cost a lot of money.) I place the bracelet behind my back and focus on Peppa, telling Reese in soothing tones how tired I am, how tired Peppa is, and how Milo is already snoring. I turn on her sound machine and the night-light and watch as she closes her eyes.

Bingo. I close the door behind me just as Mom is walking up to Reese's room with a picture book. I can see the dark rings under her eyes. When she came in earlier, I heard her on the phone with someone talking about a mix-up with a press release she had to do and it sounds like she had a rough day. I wave her away.

"She's asleep," I whisper.

Mom looks stunned. "You truly are the baby whisperer." She hugs me. "What would I do without you?"

This is my moment! I can feel it. I usher Mom toward the stairs. "I don't know. I'm very reliable, which is why I really think Ava and I can handle a dog-walking business."

"Harper," Mom says with a deep sigh that sends up red flags, but I can't stop now. I think again of Ava's text. I need to tell them why I want this and go for it.

I follow Mom into the kitchen. "I know you think I'm not ready, but look at how good I am with Reese and Milo."

Dad comes around the corner carrying an assortment of Reese's toys on top of a basket of laundry. He sees me and must see the look on my mom's face because he stops short. He looks tired too. "What's going on?"

"She wants to talk about dog walking again," Mom tells Dad as if I'm not even in the room. Dad makes a face.

I feel indignant. "What's wrong with dog walking? It's the perfect first job!"

"It's a lot of responsibility," Dad starts to say.

"I'm very responsible," I point out. Yet again. "Look at how I am with Reese and Milo. I'm the most responsible twelve-and-a-half-year-old I know."

"If you're that responsible, then we shouldn't have to remind you to unload the dishwasher," Mom says as she turns to the machine in question and motions to the magnet on the front that says "I'm clean," which means "Unload me now!"

"Or put away your laundry," Dad adds.

Uh-oh. The tide is turning. I feel like I'm forgetting all the words I planned on saying. I know I had some good "talking points," as Ava calls them, but for the life of me, they've gone out of my head. "I do my chores, but sometimes when I'm trying to do homework and I'm helping out with Reese—"

"She's your sister," Mom cuts in. "Don't you want to play with her?"

"Of course, but—"

"You're twelve," Dad adds. "We don't think it's so much to ask you to keep an eye on her sometimes."

"I know, but—" *Let me speak!* I want to say. I just don't know what I want to actually say other than I can do this. Please let me. But that approach has never worked in the past with social media or the movies or the mall. I need something stronger. "If you'd just let me explain why I'm ready . . ."

Mom throws a dish towel into the sink. "Harper, it's been a long day. Didn't we already cave and give in to you being on social media today?"

"Yes, but—" I try to argue.

"So why are you pushing it?" Mom says, an edge to her voice. "This is not the time to talk about this on your way out the door."

"I know, but Ava—" I try again.

This just gets Mom more upset. "Harper! Enough! Just go to Celia's party and have a good time, okay?" Her voice softens. "We'll pick you and Ava up at ten." She turns back to Dad to talk about some show they plan on binging while I'm out.

I feel a twinge of annoyance creep up inside me. Why can't they listen to me? I bet Blake's parents paid attention when she explained why she was leaving college to start her career. They probably didn't say she was too young for everything she wanted to try. I hear my phone ping and see Ava running up my walk.

"Hey!" she says. "How'd it go?"

"It didn't." I shut the door behind me, not even saying goodbye to my parents, which I feel bad about, but I'm too upset.

"Harper!" Ava moans. "We went over all your talking points at lunch today. Your argument was solid. Why didn't you talk to them?"

"I tried," I tell her, feeling myself start to get annoyed. Why does Ava have to act like my mom sometimes? "They shut me down the minute I brought it up."

"So you keep trying!" Ava insists. "My mom wasn't sure about the business at first, but then when I told her how they could have the contact info for every family we dog walk, she was like, this sounds great and . . ."

"My parents are always busy with Reese," I remind her. "Tonight my mom and dad were so tired from work they wouldn't even let me open the conversation. I tried. Really."

I hear Ava give a deep sigh. "Not hard enough. If you really wanted to do this with me, you'd make it happen. You're always so afraid to stand up for yourself."

"Just stop!" I feel hot tears spring to my eyes. I hate when Ava says things like this. She's an only child. She doesn't see how another sibling can suck up all the air in the room. "I wish you'd stop pushing me."

Ava stares at me, stunned. I've gone too far, I know, but I can't help myself. Doesn't Ava see I want my parents to let me grow up? But I don't say that. Ava doesn't say anything either. Her mom's car idles in the driveway, but neither of us moves to get in.

Finally Ava's mom yells out the window. "Girls? Are you coming?"

Ava and I don't look at each other. I hear my phone ping.

Zach

You're up to 958 likes on your video!!!

My mood instantly lifts. People like me! Before I think better of it, I squeal and look at Ava. "Guess what? My Taylor video has nine hundred and fifty-eight likes since this morning!"

Ava looks at me incredulously. "That's what you're excited about right now? Your TikTok? I guess you really don't care about our dog-walking business."

I gape. "No, I—"

"Just forget it," Ava snaps. "I don't even want to go into business together. I'm going to do it on my own."

"Fine!" I say, feeling shaky. The evening is going downhill, and it hasn't even started yet. I move to get in the car and away from my best friend. Ava's mom smiles the minute she sees me.

"Hi, Harper! Ready for Celia's party?"

"Yep, thanks for driving me," I say, suddenly feeling awkward. Ava is staring out the window, ignoring me and her mom now. My hands are still shaking from the conversation I just had with my parents and now Ava. This has been the weirdest half birthday ever. High points: TikTok, Zach's gift, and Celia. Low: Everything else.

My head just feels so crowded and loud these days, like I can't quiet all my thoughts and feelings. There's just so many things competing for my attention. Reese is driving me bonkers. My parents are treating me like a baby. Seventh grade is weird. I like Zach but can't tell him because it would mess up our friendship with Ava (who probably doesn't even know about the other gift Zach got me). She's obsessed with us starting a business together when I can't even get my mom to let me go to the mall alone. Some days I'm exhausted before I walk out the door. I bet Blake Riley never had days like this. She was probably already awesome, beautiful, and popular at twelve and a half.

I really should have made that half-birthday wish. I'd wish all this drama away.

"We're here!" Ava's mom announces in what feels like no time at all. I look out the window and see we're pulling into the driveway in front of a sleek black building with a glowing sign that says "Sugar Crazy" in bright pink neon lights. "Wow, this place looks cool. You girls are going to have so much fun tonight."

Ava and I glance at each other, then quickly look away, exiting from opposite car doors.

I'm not sure what Ava's plan is, but I'm going to have fun if it kills me.

5

● ● ●

This place has a wall made out of Skittles. That's the first thing I notice when Ava walks into the restaurant ahead of me. They also have walls made out of Snickers, lollipops, gumballs, and M&M's. Even the plain white walls are decorated with oversized portraits of celebrities made out of candy. From the entryway, I can see the tables are packed with people sipping brightly colored drinks that smoke or are brimming with floating gummy candy, lit sparklers, and cotton candy. A waiter carrying tie-dyed burgers passes us, and I have to resist grabbing one off the tray. I see a hostess in a neon-pink Sugar Crazy dress wave Ava and me forward, but the music is so loud, I can't hear her what she's saying. It doesn't help that there is also a waterfall behind the hostess stand spewing what looks like purple soda.

"WE'RE HERE FOR CELIA DARROW'S PARTY!"

I try, and the hostess nods knowingly. She grabs two brightly colored menus and motions to us to follow her. I'm practically giddy as we make our way to a glass-walled room. The hostess swings open the door. "Your final guests have arrived," she announces.

I pause. Final guests? My face burns as I look around the room and see a dozen girls already seated at the table. They all look up and stare at us. All the spots near Celia are taken.

"Harper, Ava, hello! Thanks for coming!" Mrs. Darrow walks over to us, and a cloud of floral perfume follows. She's dressed in booties and slim jeans with a logo top similar to one I've seen Celia wear.

"Hi, Mrs. Darrow," I say warmly. I can still remember her making the best grilled cheese sandwiches and cutting the crusts off for me when I was four. I've always hated sandwich crust.

"It's so good to see you, Harper. It's been too long." She reaches into a pricy designer bag on her shoulder and hands us plastic candy boxes with tiny silver scoops attached. The Sugar Crazy logo is stamped in neon pink on the front. "These favors are for the two of you. After dinner, you'll each get to fill your candy boxes in the Sugar Crazy store."

"Thank you," I say, staring down at the box. When

I looked at the Sugar Crazy website this afternoon, I read the candy boxes cost fifteen dollars to fill. I can't believe Celia's mom got us each one on top of paying for dinner. Plus booked a private room. My stomach does a quick somersault as I think about how different Celia's full birthday is from my own, which normally involves takeout and a movie on demand at home with Ava and Zach.

"Harper, hi!" Celia says giving me a wave.

I'm relieved to see she remembers I'm coming, I make a beeline straight for her. Ava follows, and we both hand her birthday cards. Mine has a gift card my mom bought her to the coffee place in town. It was my idea—Celia is always posting pictures at the place, so hopefully she'll like it.

"That's so sweet. Thank you," Celia says as the other girls watch the exchange. "You didn't have to get me anything."

"Of course we did," I answer for both of us as Ava is saying nothing. "It's your birthday!"

Celia laughs, and it sounds real—not fake, like I'm sure Ava is expecting. "I guess that's why we're here, right? But hey, it's your half birthday, so we can celebrate you too. I was just telling the girls about your family tradition."

"You were?" I say, unable to hide my surprise. Celia was talking about me? Is that a good thing?

"Yes! I love that your family celebrates you twice a year," Celia says, her smile widening, and I feel my stomach unclench. "Mom, did I tell you Harper even gets presents?"

I'm not sure Mrs. Darrow hears Celia. She's on the phone with someone.

"Half-birthday presents?" Celia's best friend, Saya, gasps. "I need to get in on this."

Celia motions to Saya and everyone else to move down a seat so that I can sit next to her. *Me.* I stare at the empty seat for a second, feeling as confused as Saya looks. Celia pats the purple chair. "Tell us everything!"

I look from the seat to Ava. There's nowhere for her to sit.

"I'll just be down there," Ava says flatly, motioning to the empty end of the table. No one tries to stop her.

I glance at the seat next to Celia again. Then I look at Ava's retreating figure. Do I follow Ava or sit here, in the hot seat?

Celia pats the purple chair again. "Are you going to sit down? We have a lot to talk about." She fiddles with the silver puzzle-piece charm around her neck. I notice all the other Cambridge Street Girls have on the same necklace.

I wish I had a puzzle-piece charm necklace too. I touch the bracelet on my wrist that Zach and Ava gave me. They did not get identical ones. Maybe I should suggest they do so we can look more like a group too.

Heart pounding, I sit down, trying not to smile too much because inside all I can think is *Celia says we have a lot to talk about!*

"So . . . ," Celia says, leaning in close. "How did you do it?"

The other girls look at me. I glance at Ava, who is doing something on her phone, or at least pretending to. "Do . . . what?"

Celia starts to laugh. Saya does too, and then the other girls chime in.

"Get so many likes!" Celia says.

"Likes?" I repeat, still not understanding. I thought they wanted to talk about my half birthday.

"On TikTok!" Saya says. "We noticed you just posted your first video today and you have over a thousand likes."

"And it's only been up for half a day," another girl marvels. "I've never had more than two hundred likes."

"So?" Saya leans in, her hand resting on her chin, giving me a view of her manicure, which is the same lavender shade as Celia's. "How'd you do it?"

"I don't know," I admit. "I guess people like Taylor Swift."

"Duh," says Saya. "But lots of people use that song in videos. Why is yours going viral?"

Everyone pulls out their phone to see the video for themselves and I can hear "22" playing faintly around the room.

"You know what I think it is?" Celia pipes up. "You're no robot—just dancing around or plugging a product. This is so different." She gets to the part of me applying candy-apple-red lipstick while singing the song. "I haven't seen anyone lip-synch while applying makeup and telling you where to buy similar products that are cheap. And you make it all look so easy." She eyes me appraisingly. "You have to help me do one of these."

"These . . . ?" I question.

"Makeup videos!" Celia says. "I don't want to copy yours, of course, so we can do mine differently, but I'd love to get more followers. I barely have a thousand."

"A thousand?" I say in awe. For some reason, I don't mention I'm up to over a thousand followers myself, even though I so want to.

"Celia's videos are the best," says one of two Heathers in attendance. (They look similar, but I've always been able to keep them straight because Heather Number 1 likes to wear her hair in a ponytail.)

"*The* best!" says Heather Number 2, who stares at me as if to dare me to disagree. The other girls around the table nod, reminding me of Dad's bobblehead collection. Reese is always patting the heads of the figures to make them move.

Everyone is staring at me. Oh, am I supposed to say it too? "The best!" I agree, and everyone's shoulders seem to relax.

"WHOA," Saya says. "Harper, you've got one thousand three hundred followers!"

"I do?" I say, trying not to sound too excited, because I already knew this and Celia is staring at me. But I *am* excited. People love my video!

"All from one post!" Saya says in amazement.

All the Cambridge Street Girls look at me as if I'm a creature in the science lab they're studying.

"You have to do a video for me," Celia declares, her brown eyes rimmed with gray liner piercing mine. "Right away! Can you come over after school tomorrow and bring all your makeup and equipment to shoot it?"

Me? Hang out on Cambridge Street with the Cambridge Street Girls? "Yes!" I say without thinking. At the other end of the table, I see Ava frown, but I ignore it.

"Perfect," Celia says. "Maybe I should use '22' too."

But I already used "22," I want to say, but don't. I don't want Celia getting annoyed. Instead, I find myself saying, "You could."

"I bet Blake Riley will like whatever you post," Saya says.

Celia beams. "Can you guys imagine if she started following me after the video Harper does? We have to tag her in the post."

"She will follow you!" says Heather 1.

"Definitely!" says Heather 2, and all the girls agree.

I can't help but glance at Ava again. I know her well enough to know exactly what she's thinking: the Cambridge Street Girls are clones. But I don't see it that way. They're being really nice to me even though I'm not one of the CSGs. Looking around, I notice most of the girls are wearing their hair the same way—down like Celia with barrel-rolled curls. I touch my shorter hair self-consciously. Maybe I could grow my hair out too. And get a good curling iron. Mom always worries Reese will get ahold of it and burn herself, but I can hide it when I'm not using it. Still, if I was older and lived alone, I wouldn't have these problems.

"I guess we should decide what we want to order." Celia smiles at me apologetically. "Harper, do you mind if Saya sits next to me again? We were going to share fries."

"Yay, we're sharing fries." Saya sounds way too territorial about fried food.

"Sure." I feel my face warm again despite me willing it not to. "I should go sit by Ava anyway."

"Talk more later!" Celia says. "And I'll text you my address for tomorrow."

"Great!" I know where she lives. We used to have playdates at her house all the time in preschool. But no matter. I'm going to Celia's! I practically float to the other end of the table, listening to everyone decide what they're having to eat.

Ava doesn't look up as I sit down next to her. I feel bad about ditching her back there. I'm sure Celia didn't mean to leave her out, but it was weird she didn't acknowledge Ava.

"Hey," I whisper, holding my menu up so no one can hear us. "What are you getting? Want to split fries?"

Ava gives me a look. "Acting like a CSG clone already?"

"No," I say, flustered. "I was trying to be funny."

"Yeah." Ava looks back at her menu. "This is so funny, watching you fawn over Celia, trying to get her to like you."

That's not fair, I want to say. "She was the one talking to me."

"About you doing a video for *her,*" Ava says. "Feels like she's using you, if you ask me."

The words hit like a gut punch. "Well, I didn't ask you," I whisper hotly. "You're just jealous because she's acting like you're not even here." I see Ava's face fall, and immediately regret what I've said. "Ava—"

"Forget it," she snaps, looking down. "And no, I don't want to split fries."

"Everything okay over there?"

I put down my menu and see Heather 1 staring at us. Ava won't look up, but I've always been bad at silences. I can hear Saya asking Celia a million questions at the fun end of the table. ("What are you ordering? Are you getting mayo on your burger? What flavor milkshake are you getting?") I'm tired just hearing her hang on Celia's every answer. But, you know, I do kind of want to order what everyone else is ordering.

"Yep!" I say cheerily. "Just not sure what to get. What are you getting . . . Heather?" Both Heathers look up.

70

"The tie-dye burger," they say at the same time.

A waitress appears with Rice Krispies Treat sushi. I take one.

"Me too," I say automatically, and I hear Ava sigh again. "It's supposed to be great," I add defensively. Why shouldn't I get the best thing on the menu if it's good? Isn't that the whole point of trying out popular menu items?

"You've never been here?" Heather 1's head tilts in my direction, and I watch her ponytail swish.

"You *have* to have been here before," Heather 2 adds, as if I'm lying.

"Nope," I say, and stuff the treat in my mouth. "First time."

"Huh," Heather 2 says and looks at Heather 1.

"Then how did your mom get the reservation for Celia?" Heather 1 asks.

"My mom?" I lean in closer, wondering if I misheard her over the loud music. Ava looks up at me worriedly.

"How did your mom score Celia's reservation?" Heather 1 says slower this time. I notice a few other girls look over the tops of their brightly colored menus.

"My mom?" I repeat, still confused. My heart is starting to beat fast again. I have a sinking feeling in my chest. What does my mom have to do with this?

"Celia said your mom knows someone who runs this place and they got Ce-Ce's mom the reservation since it's so impossible to get in here." Heather 1 grabs a piece of Rice Krispies sushi.

"I heard Celia's mom made her invite you since you scored the reservation," Heather 2 adds, a small smile playing on her lips. "Birthday dinners are usually a Cambridge Street Girls–only kind of thing."

6

The music in the room suddenly feels too loud, and I sense staring at me. I hear Saya laugh, and I'm sure it's about me.

NO.

Mom wouldn't push Mrs. Darrow to invite me to Celia's party . . . would she?

I think back to our conversation this morning in the car: my mom said Celia's mom called and invited *us.* Yes. That's what happened. My mom didn't push for us to get invited tonight. Unless . . . My heart is beating faster as I remember Ava's reaction about it not making sense. If Celia wanted to invite us, why didn't she just do it herself? If Celia really wanted to hang out, would she pick her birthday party dinner to do it at?

Maybe she's just being nice to you because her mom told her to.

But why would Celia invite me to her house to do a TikTok, then?

Feels like she's using you, if you ask me, I hear Ava say again.

Looking around the table, I know now for certain Heather 2 is right—Ava and I are the only non–Cambridge Street Girls here. We aren't part of this group. We don't talk at school. Celia didn't want me here, and everyone knows it. I feel like such a fool. My head starts to spin, and I'm certain I'm going to toss the Rice Krispies sushi I just consumed. *Don't throw up. Don't throw up.* The room begins to feel too small. I have to get out of here.

I stand up fast, my chair scraping against the floor. "Where is the bathroom?" I ask.

Heather 2 points to the glass doors, watching me closely. "We're about to order, though. Don't you want to wait?"

"I'll be right back," I say, smiling too wide as I walk fast to the door.

"Harper," I think I hear Ava say, but I ignore her too.

I don't want to hear her say *I told you so.* Celia smiles and I attempt a smile back, but I can't manage actual words.

Celia didn't want you here. You are not friends.

Celia didn't invite you.
Celia didn't invite you.
Celia didn't invite you.

The words are vibrating in my head like the song playing way too loud in the restaurant. I'm shaking I'm so mad at Mom, myself, Ava for being right, Reese for being such a wrecker, my life for being my life. I push open the glass door, spinning around till I see a sign for the restrooms. Ava is still calling my name, but I walk faster, not stopping till I see the women's room. Praying it's not occupied, I turn the handle, then quickly lock the door behind me. It's a single with the strangest wallpaper I've ever seen. Are those black-and-white silhouettes of people dancing? It doesn't matter. The room muffles the sounds of the outside world and everyone in it. I lean back against the door and feel the tears begin to fall.

Celia didn't invite you.

My phone buzzes, and I'm momentarily startled by a text.

GMA

Go you and your TikTok! A thousand and four hundred and fifty followers already! My popular granddaughter!

I cringe. But I'm not popular. I'm not a Cambridge Street Girl. I'm anything but cool.

A knock at the door makes me jump.

"Harper?" Ava says quietly. "It's me."

I can't speak. I have no words that won't come out as a sob. I'm too embarrassed. Ava was right. I was wrong and I hate it.

"Open up, Harper, please? I want to talk to you."

I close my eyes, as if that will block out her voice. It doesn't. My phone buzzes in my hand again, and I'm forced to open my eyes and look at the screen. Grandma, now isn't the time. . . .

Ava

I know you're in there! Just talk to me!

Ava

Please?

Ava

It's okay, H. Really.

> Who needs the CSGs? Let's call my mom and get out of here!

And go where? I want to say. I am not going home. I can see my future: Mom and I getting into a massive fight over what happened tonight. Mom not wanting to talk because we might wake up Reese. Me caving and not saying how I can never show my face at school again. How am I going to look at those girls tomorrow? Or even when I head back to the table tonight? I'm mortified.

I can see the school year ahead of me, and I know I'll never be able to live this moment down. I'll forever be the girl whose mom forced Celia's mom to invite her to her thirteenth birthday party. This story will be the talk of the school. I bet it's one people will still be talking about when we're in high school!

High school . . . Just the thought makes me groan. Years of awkwardness ahead of me trying to be popular and failing. I just wish I could skip it all and go straight into my twenties. Those are supposed to be the best years of your life. Taylor Swift can't be wrong about that.

My phone buzzes once more. *Enough, Ava! I'm not opening the door no matter how hard you knock.*

Zach

How's it going?

I blink, the words of Zach's text swirling in front of my eyes. Did Ava text him and tell him what happened? When Zach hears, he's going to think I'm so lame.

Zach

You okay?

With shaky hands, I click over to TikTok wanting to think about anything but what's happening. Down the rabbit hole I go, scrolling through my feed till I see a new post from Blake Riley. I stop and watch. There's a slight blue hue to the video. She must be using one of those new filters Zach was talking about. I watch as Blake dances around the room applying lip gloss. Her hair looks a lot like the Cambridge Street Girls'— curled expertly—and she's wearing the cutest dress ever. Blake's clearly in her apartment, which has almost three-sixty views of downtown Los Angeles. "New Spokesperson of Mod Beauty!" flashes across the post. "So excited to be their spokeswoman! (At least till I have my own company and someday I WILL!")

I have no doubt about that. Blake is twenty-two, her life is completely her own, and it is perfection. I watch her video again, thinking about how she looks like she owns the world. I want to be just like her.

Ignoring the texts piling up, and Ava outside the bathroom door, I start to scroll through the new effects' filters, looking for the one Blake must have used in this video.

No, I don't want to be a cat. No, I don't want to have fireworks exploding behind my head. I want to be Blake! I want to be blue! I . . . oh. I pause on a filter with sparkly edges that look like stars. Is this the filter Zach meant? Its name is Birthday Wish. Would a half birthday count? I still never made my wish today. I wonder.

There's another knock at the door just as my phone buzzes again. A text pops up from my mom. I can only see the first line. *Harper, I'm sorry I . . .*, but I don't want to hear it. I swipe my mom away just like I imagine swiping away Ava's voice outside the door, Celia not inviting me, and Zach knowing what a nobody I am. I don't care if this is just a silly filter. I'm making a half-birthday wish.

I snap a selfie and close my eyes. "I wish I was twenty-two and just like Blake Riley and . . ." I pause, thinking. "I had really great hair." And then, just for good measure, I blow out the imaginary candles on an imaginary cupcake, knowing I'm a total doofus and a birthday filter wish is even goofier.

I open my eyes. Nothing's changed. Shocker.

The lights in the bathroom flicker, and I hear the music in the restaurant cut out. Before I know what's happening, I'm plunged into darkness.

7

● ● ●

The lights flicker to life again, and I realize right away
I am no longer in the bathroom.

I'm in bed!

How did that happen?

I blink hard several times, wondering if I'm dreaming. I don't remember leaving the bathroom, getting
home or even what happened with Mom. Did we
fight? Did I talk to Ava? Say anything to Celia? I don't
remember anything! All I know is my head hurts like
it does when I've been at swim practice and haven't
drunk any water.

I sit up and stretch, looking for the lump that is
Milo under the covers on my bed, but I don't see
one. Huh. Maybe he slept downstairs. Sometimes he
loves to lounge on the cold tile in the kitchen. My
room is dark, but I can make out the clock on my

desk across from the bed. It says 6:57 a.m. The house is unusually quiet, and it's never at this hour. Did Reese sleep in? If they don't get going, we'll all be late today.

Maybe that's not such a bad thing. I'm not sure I can face the world after last night.

Celia didn't invite you.

The thought comes roaring back to me, and I'm afraid I'm going to be sick. I don't know what to do about this afternoon. Do I still go to Celia's to help her with her video, or did our moms press her to ask me to do that too? Maybe I should see if Celia texted me.

I reach for my phone, which I always fall asleep next to like it's a security blanket. (I don't still have one of those. Nope.) But my phone isn't where it usually is, and I can't find it tangled in the sheets either. I roll out of bed onto the floor to check under my bed and—*Cough! Wheeze!* Dust bunnies! Maybe Mom was right about this room needing a cleaning. Either way, the phone isn't under there either.

"Where is my phone?" I grumble.

"Good morning, Harper!" someone says, and I jump, banging my head underneath the bed in surprise. "Your phone is located in your bag."

"Oww!" I say, pulling myself out from under the bed and sitting up. "Who said that? Alexa?"

"This is Alice, your personal assistant," says a voice that sounds computer-generated.

Alice? I guess I renamed Alexa . . . but wait a minute. When did Mom get me an Alexa? And since when did it have a Find My Phone feature?

"The temperature today is sixty-nine degrees going up to a high of seventy-six degrees," the voice continues. "There will be partly cloudy skies with a chance of an afternoon shower during the hours of one and two p.m., when you have your walk-through of tonight's event at Fenway Park."

"Fenway Park?" I repeat. "Dad got tickets to a game on a school night?" Usually we are a weekend-games-only kind of family during the school year.

"Today you have three meetings—a breakfast with Blake at nine, a team meeting at eleven, and your walk-through at one p.m. before hair and makeup come at four-thirty for the event," the voice says. "Should I cancel your morning alarm since you're already up?"

"Hair and makeup? For me?" I look for the small crossbody bag I used last night for the party but don't see that either. Instead, I see a large butter-yellow leather bag made by a very expensive brand sitting on my desk. Is that Mom's? Maybe Alexa—I'm sorry, *Alice*—meant my phone is in there. I search inside the bag, but all I find is a bunch of makeup still in its packaging and a tablet of some kind.

"No phone!" I tell Alice.

"You should get going," she says. "At seven-twenty-five a.m., it will take an hour to get into the city and you need time to park."

Park? Okay, this device is definitely wonky. Maybe it's crossed signals with a neighbor's device. I choose to ignore it and stumble to my closet to find clothes to wear to school. Yawning, I turn on the closet light and shriek. "Sweet Cheez-Its, where are my clothes?"

My closet has been transformed into a pantry! My clothes have been replaced with a vacuum, two cases of paper towels, a box of toilet paper, and what looks like an entire closet full of nonperishables and towels.

"Would you like me to purchase something via Sky-Mail? I can have something here in . . . fifteen minutes if you order within the next sixty seconds."

What is SkyMail? I hold my head trying to stop the throbbing.

"I'm dreaming," I tell myself. "Definitely dreaming."

Alexa/Alice isn't making any sense. Forget it. I'll

84

just wear what I have on. It's not like I haven't worn pajamas to school before, although I don't remember owning pink satin shorts and a button-down short-sleeved pajama top. Maybe Mom or Dad has seen my phone. I step into the hall. It's dark and quiet, like it's still the middle of the night.

"Mom?" I call, walking down the hall to their room and finding it empty. Their bed is made as if they haven't slept in it. "Dad?" I go to Reese's room. Maybe they're in there getting her dressed. "You guys in— WHOA!" I jump back in surprise.

Reese's crib is gone! Instead there is a full-sized bed decorated with half a dozen squishy pillows shaped like rainbows and ice cream cones and posters from movies I don't recognize. There's also a string of fairy lights holding photographs.

"What is going on?" I ask the universe. I don't expect a reply, but I get one from a voice I don't recognize.

"What's going on is we're going to be late if you don't get going."

I turn around. A girl about my own age is glaring at me. She has curly dark brown hair, a round face, and eyes so big they look like saucers. She looks vaguely familiar. "Who are you?"

She rolls her eyes. "Funny. Because we haven't seen each other in months. I get it." She crosses her arms. "Why aren't you dressed? I thought you had to leave at seven-thirty for your 'big day.'" She uses air quotes for the words "big day."

"Big day?" Why am I so confused this morning?

"Okay, so maybe Fenway is not a big deal to you, but we thought it sounded cool, even if you didn't find us worthy of an invite." Her fingers brush the hallway wall and I notice her chipped blue nail polish.

Who is this person in my house that somehow knows me and Alice's Fenway plan? Maybe I did hit my head in the bathroom. "An invite? Do you mean to the swim meet against Concord? That's not till next week. My parents usually don't come to away meets because it's hard with Reese."

The girl blinks hard. "Did you hit your head or something? Do you need me to get Mom?"

"Mom?" I am suddenly very aware of the crinkle in the girl's forehead and the dot of freckles across her nose. I get the eeriest of feelings. *I know this girl.* She almost looks like she could be . . . *no.* That's impossible, but I say it anyway. "Reese?" I whisper.

"Who else would I be?" she says.

I start to hyperventilate. This is my sister! My baby

sister! In my head I see a two-year-old with chubby fingers toddling around my room, breaking lipsticks and yelling "I SEE IT?" anytime she spots my phone. "But you're so old!"

She snorts. "Look who's talking, Grandma."

"Grandma?" I touch my face in horror. It feels normal, but nothing else is this morning. Am I ancient? I run for the upstairs bathroom in a panic.

And start screaming.

Reese comes running in after me as I duck down from the mirror, holding on to the bathroom vanity for support. Slowly, I stand up again and face the mirror.

The face I'm looking at is mine . . . but not. It's older. Way older, but not *old*. I touch my face, smooshing my cheeks together. The girl staring back at me has got to be ten years older than me. She's like an actual adult! But a cool adult. She's got great hair (even her bedhead has perfect spiral curls). Her skin is dewy and has a slight tan to it like she's been out in the sun, and she's got curves rather than a beanpole for a torso. I bet she can even do that new TikTok dance everyone is doing.

I try to do it myself for fun and the girl in the reflection does it perfectly! "It's me," I realize.

Reese is standing in the doorway watching me. "Okay, you're really acting weird. I'm getting Mom."

"No!" I grab her wrist. "How old am I?"

Reese's eyebrow crinkle again. "Twenty-two and a half today, which is how Mom convinced you to sleep over last night. So we could celebrate your half birthday this morning before your event."

Nope. Not possible. I start to hyperventilate again, taking gulping breaths. "I'm twelve and a half. We celebrated this morning!"

"*I'm* twelve and a half," Reese clarifies. "You're twenty-two and a half."

I slump against the wall next to the towel rack. It takes me a second to realize the floral wallpaper we had in the room is gone and has been replaced by the palest of blue paints. "I'm twenty-two," I repeat, trying the number on for size. "I'm twenty-two," I say again, louder this time. I start to laugh. "I'm twenty-two!"

Suddenly I remember the half-birthday wish I made on the TikTok filter last night in Sugar Crazy.

That couldn't have worked . . . could it?

Nope. I'm dreaming. This has to be the longest dream I've ever had, but if it's real, I don't have to worry about Celia's party anymore or whether to pretend I'm sick to get out of going to school. I'm twenty-two! All that stuff is in the past! And look at

88

twenty-two-year-old me: I have a Blake Riley vibe going on. This is incredible!

"Harper! Reese!" Mom's distinctive voice comes drifting up the stairs, and I jump. "We have to get going! Are you two coming downstairs?"

"Yes!" I feel slaphappy, like I've had one too many Red Vines.

"Maybe I should go get Mom," Reese says, sounding concerned.

"No, I'll come downstairs, and we can celebrate me being twenty-two and a half," I say with glee. This is probably a dream, but why not go with it and see where it takes me? I rush past Reese down the stairs and into the kitchen. I stop short when I see my parents.

They look older too but not alarmingly so. Mom's got a few laugh lines around the eyes and Dad's hairline seems to have receded slightly, but they still look very much like Mom and Dad. Mom smiles when she sees me. "Happy half birthday!" she says, pulling me into a hug.

For the slightest of seconds, I freeze, thinking about the whole Celia thing again. My head is yelling, *I'm really mad at you, Mom!* but Dream Me has to remind myself that's so ten years ago! So I hug her too. "Thanks!"

"We're going to sing, but you only texted me you could come late last night, so I didn't have time to get you a cake," Mom says apologetically. "We had a rainbow cake sent to your apartment."

"My apartment?" I say, flabbergasted. "I don't live here?"

Mom and Dad laugh. "You're still so funny," Dad says, side-hugging me. "I've missed you, kid. Don't be such a stranger."

I have an apartment! My own space! No one forcing me to do chores or tell me if I can hang out with my friends on a school night. I make my own rules! I sigh blissfully. This dream is the best one ever!

"How come you're not dressed yet?" Mom asks. "Didn't you say you had to leave at seven-thirty?"

Before I can respond, I hear barking. It sounds hoarse. When I look down, Milo is waddling toward me. He's gained weight and his face is all white, but it's him.

"Milo!" I exclaim. "You're old!" I go to pick him up and he snaps at me. "Hey! Why is he growling at me?"

Reese picks him up. "He hasn't seen you since Christmas," she says, snuggling with him as he glares at me from her arms. "I think he's still holding a grudge."

"Christmas?" I question. "But it's May fifteenth. You mean I haven't been home in five months?" They all laugh.

"Very funny! You know exactly what day it is— you've been talking about May fifteenth forever!" Dad says.

"What matters is you're here now." Mom kisses my cheek. "We know our girl is super successful and has an incredibly busy career!"

"I do?" I look at them in awe. "Tell me more! What do I do now?" They can't stop laughing.

Reese rolls her eyes. "As if you need us to remind you. It's all you talk about."

"Really? Like what?" Dream Me wants to hear everything!

Mom hugs me again. "Next time you come, we'll definitely do dinner and celebrate all your accomplishments."

"Yeah, if you can get here early enough and not come in and go right to bed." Dad motions to the pot of coffee.

"Eww. No way," I say, backing away from the pot. Even the smell of coffee turns my stomach. "Do you have any chocolate milk?"

"Milk? You drink like three cups of coffee a day!" Dad exclaims. Reese is staring at me strangely.

Beep! Beep! Beep! Beep! "The time is now seven-twenty-four, and the car is fully charged," says a cheery British accent. "House alarm being set in fifteen minutes. Shall I proceed?"

"Yes," Mom says. "Okay, everyone out. Oh! Wait. Harper, should we sing? Or put on our lipstick and dance to Taylor's '32'?"

"You mean '22,'" I tell her.

"No, I mean '32.'" Mom looks at Reese questioningly. "Isn't that a song on Taylor's latest album?"

"How should I know?" Reese says, and motions to me. "Ask Harper. She's the one who just got back from Cabo with her."

"I went on vacation with Taylor Swift?" I scream.

"Fourteen minutes," says the house.

"Okay, no time for singing," Mom says, kissing me again. "Good seeing you, honey. We can't wait to see coverage of the event! It sounds amazing. You should get dressed, though. If the house locks with you in it, you won't be able to unlock it for thirty minutes and you'll be late. Aren't you meeting Blake at nine?" She heads out of the kitchen, and I hear the garage door open.

There is so much about that sentence that doesn't

compute. Who is Blake? And even more importantly: "I'm driving myself"? *Me?*

Dad opens the front blinds and motions to the sports car out front. "Yes, and you're going to hit a lot of traffic if you don't get going. Did you forget to charge your car last night?"

I look outside at the bright blue convertible. "That's mine?" Squee! Dream Me is living large!

"Give my love to the team!" Dad says. "Coming, Reese?"

"Yep!" Reese says, and hands me the yellow bag from my room. Apparently, it's mine! "Well, see ya. I guess we'll see you at Mom's birthday in October or online in *Vogue* first."

Vogue? Me? "Why would I be in *Vogue*?" I question.

Reese backs away from me. "You're always in *Vogue*. Between the makeup lines and the parties, you are featured everywhere."

"Right." I pause. "And *Vogue* covers me because I wear makeup?"

Reese's eyes nearly bulge out of her head. "You are the head of marketing for Blake's Face of Beauty makeup company!"

"I am?" My heart is beating wildly as I slowly start to understand what my family is talking about. "Wait.

Do you mean Blake as in Blake Riley?" Reese nods. "I work for Blake Riley's company? She has a company? And I know her and work for her?" The words coming out of my mouth make zero sense, but Reese is nodding away as if they do. I scream with wild excitement, and Reese holds her ears. "*Me*. You're sure about this? I know Blake Riley?"

"Yeah, and I'm pretty sure you just call her 'Blake,'" she says.

I do a happy dance right there in the kitchen with a variation of the running man thrown in. Reese looks alarmed.

"Um, Harper? You're freaking me out."

"Reese! Harper!" Mom calls. "House is locking in eleven minutes! Let's go!"

The house is about to lock. I am not dressed. I can't find my phone. I have a cool car that may not be charged, and I clearly don't know how to drive. I glance at my younger sister. Reese clearly knows Dream Me, and I want to know more about this insanely bonkers, fabulous life I have before I wake up. *If* I wake up. I want to stay in this dream forever!

"WAIT!" I shout, and block Reese's exit out of the room. She looks startled. "What are you doing today?"

"Going to school," she says flatly.

"Come with me instead," I blurt out.

Her eyes widen. "You want *me* to go to work with *you*?"

"Yes! Work!" I nod. "Um, do you know how to get there? And maybe we can stop by my apartment first so I can change? If you know where I live."

Reese shakes her head. "You must be really stressed today."

"Stressed," I agree. "That's it. Because I can't find my phone."

Reese points to my head. "It's been in your ear the whole time." She reaches over and clicks something. A see-through screen pops up in midair. I immediately ooh.

"What is this thing?" I whisper.

"Your phone," Reese repeats. "And Alice."

"You know Alice?" I freak again. "She's real?"

Reese scrunches up her brow again. "Maybe I *should* come with you today."

8

Surprisingly, it doesn't take much to convince my parents to let Reese skip school.

"Spend the day with you? Of course! It will be so educational seeing how a company is run!" Mom gushes as the house locks behind us, leaving me in my silk pajamas on the front lawn.

"We can drive into the city tonight after the event and pick her up," Dad agrees. "Have a great time!" They're backing their car—a new one, I might add—out of the driveway before I can even process what just happened.

"I don't believe it," I say, watching their car drive away. "I can't even go to the mall alone, and they're letting you skip school?"

Reese looks at me. "What's a mall?"

"I'm not even sure how to respond to that." I pull

at the irritating tiny device in my ear. I keep hearing a pinging sound, but I ignore it.

"Okay, clearly something is up with you today, but since whatever is wrong means I get to go to the Fenway event and meet Blake Riley and stars like Joshua Bassett, I'm just going to go with it."

I grab her arm. "Joshua Bassett? In Boston? What about Harry Styles? Is he here too?"

"Eww," Reese says. "Harry Styles is so *old*."

"No he's . . ." Oh. I guess add ten years and he's kind of like a dad age. Still, *Harry Styles*. "But is he coming?"

"I think he's performing tonight," Reese says. "At least that's what you posted."

"He's going to SING?" I scream, and whatever new neighbor that lives across the street stops rolling their garbage can to the curb and stares at me in my pj's worriedly.

Who cares? I'm going to a party with Hollywood stars! Twenty-two is the best age ever!

Reese pulls me toward my car. "Geez, you need to calm down. It's not a big deal. You hang out with stars in Boston all the time." She pulls my bag off my arm, waves it at the car, and it unlocks.

"I do?" I ask as she leads me to the driver's seat. "Why would they want to come to Boston?"

"New York and Los Angeles are too much of a scene, so now stars live all over. There are influencer houses in every major city in the country. You know this—you've visited most of them with your job." She motions to the open car door. "Get in."

"I've been to influencer houses?" My jaw is going to permanently fall off.

"Maybe you're sick," Reese decides. "A high fever would explain this brain fart you're having." She waves to the empty driver seat again. "Get in! You're going to be late for your meeting with Blake! Didn't Alice say it was at nine?"

I stare at the car and feel my brow start to bead with sweat. I'm enjoying this all so much I don't want this dream to end, but driving? If this does turn out to be real, I don't think I can handle that part. Our neighbor is still staring at us. "See the thing is, the only driving I've done is in *Mario Kart*. And I always crash!"

"We will set the car to self-driving mode, drop it at your apartment so you can change, and then Uber the rest of the day, okay? It's easier to Uber around the city anyway." Reese leans into the car and presses some buttons.

"Self-driving?" I stare at the car curiously. "Well, if I don't have to do anything . . ." I slide into the car, breathing in the leather smell and staring at the giant touch screen on the dash. I can't believe this is mine! "Can we drive with the top down?" I squeal.

Reese closes herself in the passenger seat. "No." She presses another button, and the car begins to pull out of the spot as the top rolls up. I wave to the nosy neighbor as we drive past. "I need to be able to hear you when you tell me what's going on with you." Reese gives me a pointed look.

It's the same look she gives me whenever she's hiding one of Milo's chew toys and doesn't want me to know where it is. I know she won't stop until I tell her. "You're not going to believe me," I admit. "I'm not sure I even believe it. It's like a dream—it's everything I've ever wanted." I close my eyes and lean my head back against the headrest. "I want it to be true, but it can't be."

Reese folds her arms across her lap as the car turns onto the entrance ramp for the highway. "Explain."

I can hear my heart beating faster now. If I'm really twenty-two, I clearly need Reese's help figuring out where I need to be today. And if this is just a dream, then there's no harm done. I guess it's okay to tell her the truth, but I still blurt it out fast. "I made a half-birthday wish on my twelve-and-a-halfth birthday on a TikTok filter at Celia Darrow's party, and the next thing I knew I was twenty-two."

Reese blinks. "You're telling me you don't remember *anything* about your life from twelve and a half to twenty-two?"

"Nope!" I squeal with glee. If this is real, I don't have to worry about middle school. There is no more fighting with Mom and Dad about whether I'm old enough to do stuff on my own. I have no homework and no lousy math grades! No awkward haircuts or zits! No worrying about facing Celia and the Cambridge Street Girls after the party. I've bypassed it all and landed here in this super-sleek-looking car THAT I OWN. "Isn't it great? I skipped everything, and now I'm twenty-two!"

Reese lets this all sink in for a moment. "So you wished to be twenty-two? That's it?"

"No, I wished to be just like Blake Riley." I feel foolish saying the words out loud, but they're true. "And I wanted to be twenty-two, popular like Celia, cool, and a TikTok star . . . with great hair."

Reese's eyes bulge out of her head. "If you're telling the truth, your wish came true."

"'If you tell the truth, you don't have to remember anything,'" I say.

"Mark Twain," Reese says. "That's one of Dad's favorite quotes."

"Still?" I ask, and Reese nods. "Glad to see some things never change."

Reese stares at me, and I wonder how she's going to react. Then her face breaks into a half smirk. "You *do* have really great hair."

I touch my head and start to laugh. "So you believe me?"

Reese shrugs. "You are acting weirder than normal so . . . maybe? Half-birthday wishes are powerful. That's what Mom always says, right?"

"She does." I reach for my sister's hand since I don't have to hold the steering wheel. (Again, so weird.) "Thanks for coming. I don't think I could get through the day without you."

"Okay, now I have to believe you because that's something you've never said to me before!" Reese exclaims. "Maybe I should make better half-birthday wishes. I usually just wish for new shoes or a gift card to SkyMail."

"What's SkyMail?" I ask.

"I should actually message them right now to have an outfit waiting at your apartment," says Reese, touching her ear where her AirPod-shaped phone is. The transparent screen pops up, and then seconds later she's scrolling through screens of clothing and making choices. "I can't wear this to your event, but actually . . . hmmm . . . you're loaded, so we'll charge this to your account because I definitely need something to wear to work and then a cute dress to wear to the event at Fenway for when I talk to Olivia Rodrigo." *Ping!* Reese closes out the screen.

"She's coming too?" I gasp. "And what do you mean I'm loaded? I know I have this car and I work for Blake, but I want to know how I got here!" It's all so exciting!

"So I was little, but I think it was right after Celia's thirteenth birthday party at Sugar Crazy," Reese explains as we pass a sign on the highway that says Boston is fifteen miles ahead. I can see the Prudential sign looming in the distance. "You started posting these videos of you doing makeup looks from music videos with makeup that's affordable and easy to re-create, and the videos started blowing up. Blake took notice."

"I can't believe Blake saw them!" I say in awe. I only posted the "22" one the day of the half-birthday wish. "Then what happened?"

"You started doing all your videos with Celia under a C and H account, and *that* blew up too. That's when you started getting sponsors and media coverage and got so huge that you couldn't even go to school anymore without being mobbed," Reese recalls. "You finished high school virtually."

"I'm an influencer?" I say, my face all dreamy. I hear the pinging in my ear again but ignore it. "I can't believe it."

"An influencer and an honorary Cambridge Street Girl, as you always like to remind me. You and Celia are besties." Reese gives me an eye roll.

I swat her arm. "NO! Really? Me? A Cambridge Street Girl? And best friends with Celia?" This is getting better and better. I love being twenty-two!

"Yeah, so, the rest is history. You and Celia are now marketing directors of Blake Riley's Face of Beauty makeup brand, the most successful makeup company start-up in the world."

I open the leather bag on my lap and peek inside. I have a ton of Face of Beauty products in here. And I work for Blake's company! My heart starts to flutter it's beating so fast. What is happening? My life is better than I even wished for! "Marketing directors?" I say in awe. "So we . . . market things?"

"You create *buzz*," Reese says, touching her phone and pulling open another screen.

She googles my name—*my name!*—and a bunch of

articles and images show up. Pictures of a grown-up Celia and me with Blake on red carpets! Showcasing makeup looks on talk shows and news networks! Standing with Tom Holland. There's even a few articles about Blake's makeup event tonight at Fenway Park. Apparently, I picked the location for the event because our makeup is green and we're doing the party in front of Fenway's Green Monster wall. (Aaah, I get it!)

"Mom says you're the reason Blake does as well as she does," Reese adds as the city grows closer. "She's not wrong. You're really good at what you do even if you didn't go to college."

I stop smiling. "I didn't?"

Reese shakes her head. "You got your GED instead, and gave up swim team too. Mom and Dad flipped, but you weren't wrong. You're a major influencer!"

"I'm an influencer!" I repeat, still trying to process twenty-two-year-old me's world. "Wow, I really got everything I ever wanted."

Reese's smile waffles slightly as we head into a tunnel. "Yeah."

We're both quiet for a moment as I scroll through more images of me—*me!*—on Reese's screen, ignoring the pinging in my ear. The next thing I know, the car is rolling to a stop in front of a high-rise with all mirrored windows.

"This is you," Reese says, opening the car doors and hopping out.

"This is me?" I exclaim. "I have an apartment in this building?" I always imagined living in a high-rise. This one looks fancy!

"Yep." Reese motions for me to follow her to the door. "We can get out here, and the car will go park itself in the garage."

I step out. I'm barefoot and in pink pj's, but I hold my head up high because this is my apartment building! I live here! "You know my apartment number, right?"

"Yeah, we were here last fall," Reese says as she goes through the revolving door.

"That's a long time ago," I realize as I hurry after her and stop short in front of the doorman at the desk. "Hi! I live here! I'm Harper Lancaster."

He looks a bit rattled, but I'm sure that's because he's not used to me coming and going in pajamas. I follow Reese over to the elevator bank, where I see the buttons thankfully look like regular elevator buttons (whew!). Reese punches the button for the seventh floor, and we get into an elevator and go flying upward.

Then we head down the hall to apartment 27C. The two of us stare at the keypad on the door. Before I can ask what to do about not knowing the door code, Reese grabs my left hand's pointer finger and makes it press a button. The door slides open.

Wowza.

A tiny robot, which reminds me of something I'd see in *Star Wars*, comes zooming toward us. It looks a bit like a mini fridge on wheels with two lights on top that resemble eyes.

"Good morning, Harper!" it says, and I recognize the voice from my Alexa.

"You're Alice?" I exclaim.

"Yes, and you're pressed for time," the robot says. "Reese's SkyMail should arrive in the next five minutes, but what have you decided on wearing today?"

The robot zooms ahead of me past the living room and kitchen, and I follow, my tongue practically hanging out of my mouth. The space is all sleek modern couches, purple pillows, white area rugs, white walls—Reese the Wrecker wouldn't survive two minutes here. Neither would Milo; he'd be ripping down those funky polka-dot curtains in seconds. A large window looking out at the city is the sole light in the room, but it's bright enough that it feels like every light in the place is on. Another door slides open to reveal the bedroom.

The bedroom is huge. A beautiful queen-sized bed with turquoise linens and cute throw pillows anchors a room with soft blush-colored walls and framed black-and-white photos of buildings in Boston. Along one wall is a pristine white desk with neatly organized clear cubes holding every type of makeup applicator I can think of, along with tubes of lipstick, eye pencils, and shadows. There is a funky-looking bookcase with no books, just lots of strange sculptures and what look like trophies. In another corner is a photo shoot back-drop with an elaborate ladder-like contraption stand-ing in front of it. But what really impresses me about this room is how neat it is. There's no old gym socks on the floor or half-filled water bottles around the room. This room looks like it belongs on TV.

"This is so nice," I whisper to Reese, who just shakes her head and smirks.

I'm living the dream here!

A red laser appears on the front of the mini fridge, and it points to a wall with a picture of the famed Boston Citgo sign. The picture disappears and reveals sliding doors to a walk-in closet packed with clothes! I scream and rush into the closet behind the robot.

"As a reminder, you wore the Felicity Ralph dress three weeks ago, so it would be appropriate to wear again, or there are the packages in the front hall that have been scanned," Alice tells me. "One is the Ripped Jeans brand pair of ripped jeans that you've been waiting for. Another has a pair of sneaker boots, and another is a package from . . ." The robot pauses. "From Brand International Inc., with a note that reads: 'Harper, good chat last week with Celia! Let's make this deal happen!' Shall I fetch your packages, or would you like to wear something else?"

I don't know what to say. I own Ripped Jeans? This is the best dream ever!

"Ah, here is Reese's order," Alice says.

The robot beeps again, and I hear a whooshing sound. When I look over at my bedroom window, it's opening. A droid flies through the window with a large pink bag that it drops at my feet. Then it goes out the way it came and the window closes.

Whoa.

Reese smiles. "I'm going to change. We should get going so you're not late."

"But I don't know what to wear," I lament, biting a fingernail.

Reese pulls my finger away from my mouth. "Don't

ruin your nails! Just pick something! All your clothes are amazing, and you never share them with me."

I turn back to the closet and spy a green dress. "How about this?" I say, grabbing the hanger and staring at the price tag. I gulp. This one dress costs more than my allowance for a year!

"Nice choice," Alice comments. "You've never worn it."

I rip the tag off—such a satisfying feeling—and turn away from Alice. (I don't care if she's a robot. I get dressed alone, thank you). Then I pull off my pj top and slip on the dress. I can't help staring at my upper half for a moment, feeling somewhat impressed. "Alice, where do I keep my bras? Because I so need one, which is AWESOME!"

Bing! A drawer in the closet beeps and slides open, revealing a huge arrangement of colorful undergarments. *Bing! Bing!* Another door opens, and a rotating rack of heels comes my way. A pair that matches the dress exactly shoots out on a little platform just waiting for me to grab them. They're gorgeous and smell like new shoes, but I stare at them skeptically. Do I even know how to walk in heels? Don't I own any flats? There are none on the rotator. This is a dream. Can't I just poof them up? I scrunch my eyes tight and imagine a nice flip-flop. No, that wouldn't go with this dress. Booties? Yes! "Booties!"

"Booties went out of fashion two years ago," Alice says. "Would you like me to research the timeline of bootie fashion for your meeting today? Does this relate to the eye shadow palette you're marketing for Blake's TikTokShop?"

Blake's TikTokShop? "Uh . . ."

"Oh, and don't forget to wear your necklace," Alice adds. Another drawer opens, and a thin gold chain with a tiny round pendant appears. I pick it up and see the initials "C&H" on it. Reese appears behind me wearing a cute tee-and-skirt combo with her Vans.

"Look!" I show Reese. "Celia and I have a friendship necklace." I hug it to my chest, then put it on, dancing as I do so. This is my closet! This is my apartment! This is my life!

"Celia, yay," Reese says, and I can hear the sarcasm in her voice. I ignore it.

"Time to go," says Alice. "Fifteen minutes till your meeting with Blake."

Reese grabs my hand. "Come on, Cinderella. Let's get you to your meeting with your boss."

9

• • •

Fun fact: Ubers drive themselves in the future. And they're super tiny. Ten minutes after Alice calls for one to meet us downstairs at my fancy apartment (*my apartment!*), Reese and I are tucked inside the little car and are giving it directions to where we need to go.

"Okay, it says we need to go to 185 Newbury Street," Reese reads off my calendar, which she has up on a screen in front of us. (I swear, if she pokes my ear—aka mini phone—one more time for information, I'm going to freak out. It feels like a fly constantly buzzing around my head.)

Then Reese starts screaming. "I can't believe it! You have a breakfast meeting at One Eighty-Five?"

I stare at the shimmering screen in front of me and read my schedule again to be sure. "That's what it says. Is that a big deal?"

Reese throws herself against her seat's headrest. "Big deal? One Eighty-Five is, like, *the* restaurant in Boston! Every star goes there! And no one can get a reservation for the next two years! Wait till I tell Priyaka! I have to tell her right away!" She taps her ear, and up pops her own screen, where she begins typing so fast on the invisible screen I can't believe her digits can fly that fast. "Why aren't you flipping too? You've been there before, right?"

"Uh, no." Maybe Future Harper has, but I don't remember ever hearing of this place.

"Maybe you'll rememeber it when you see a picture." Reese swipes my calendar off the screen and pulls up an image of a plain robin's-egg-blue door of a brownstone with the numbers 185 on it.

"Looks like a normal brownstone to me." I pull down the car mirror and apply mascara. I have to say, I really like this Face of Beauty mascara called Green Lashes. It makes my lashes look way longer and thicker without going on clumpy. Apparently, all the products in my bag are part of Blake's new green line that we're launching. We! As in me! I work for Blake! I still can't believe this is happening.

"It's not," Reese insists, and slides through more

images of the interior of the restaurant and its food. "No one can get in here! No one! They only take their reservations by postcards. Can you believe? No one sends mail anymore! It's so chic."

I eye my younger sister curiously. At two, Reese the Wrecker was consumed with *Paw Patrol* and playing with my phone. But I don't know who twelve-and-a-half year-old Reese is. She seems totally comfortable in her skin, chatty, and calls things the way she sees them. So basically, the opposite of me at twelve and a half. "How do you know all this stuff?"

"I'm an entrepreneur," she says simply. "I pay close attention to the food industry. I'm *thisclose* to getting Mom and Dad to agree to let me and Priyaka get a food truck to do gourmet ice cream sandwiches for parties." She smiles, revealing a mouth full of perfect teeth.

I snort. "Yeah, great idea, but Mom and Dad will never go for it." I slather some Green Face moisturizing foundation to my face. It glides over like a light cream but has a hint of color, which I love.

"Uh, you obviously know nothing about Mom and Dad because if you did, you'd know my business plan is one they can't say no to," Reese says, chin jutted out. "Priyaka and I have the money saved for this old camper truck that is already parked at Food Truck Park near our house. They're looking for a new tenant, and it already has the freezers and everything we need to run the truck on weekend afternoons, which is when we'd have customers anyway." She points to her noggin. "Priyaka and I have been watching the crowd there for months."

"How do you have money for a camper?" I demand.

"Babysitting," Reese tells me.

"They let you babysit?" My jaw drops. "They won't even let me volunteer at a shelter."

Reese's expression falters slightly. "Yeah, well, they know they were too tough on you and it made you . . . anyway, I've just learned how to talk *to* them rather than *at* them."

"What does that mean?" I ask, miffed.

She shrugs. "I don't try to talk to them in the car or when they're distracted making dinner or laundry or stuff. I wait till they have time to talk to me and really listen, or I make them tell me when they're free to talk, and then I just lay it all out for them why I'm old enough to do these things."

"Huh." I'm always texting Mom and Dad questions and then getting mad when they say no. Or talking to them on the way to school when they're distracted. Is that why they've never listened to me? Maybe Reese is on to something here.

"But as for today, you need the code word to get into One Eighty-Five," Reese says, "and I'm guessing you don't remember it." She taps her chin. "We need your postcard." She taps my ear again before I can duck away. "Alice! Can you locate Harper's invite to One Eighty-Five?"

A voice seems to surround us in the car. "I did not create this listing. Harper manually added this reservation weeks ago, therefore I have no record of a postcard."

Is it me or does Alice sound annoyed I did this on my own?

"Okay, we'll deal with that when we get there," Reese says.

"We?" I question. "Am I allowed to just add you to the reservation?" I wonder, having flashbacks to Celia's party. "And should I be bringing my little sister to a work breakfast?"

"You need me," Reese says, her brown eyes flashing defiantly. "Whatever is going on with you, you can't take this on alone. What if Blake starts asking you questions about work and you don't know the answers? I know everything about Blake's company. I've followed her ever since you started working with her." She plays with the chipping nail polish on her fingers. "But if you want to go in alone . . ."

"No!" I say, wondering how I'm going to explain my sister coming to work on what is supposedly the biggest day of the company's career. "You should come." I hold my ear, the pinging noise getting worse and more constant. "By the way, why does my ear keep ringing?"

"Texts and messages," Reese explains. "You've been ignoring them?" She presses my phone again (grr . . .) and the screen appears once more. It's full of unopened texts and emails on either side of the screen. "Wow, you've got a lot of messages to answer."

As we're staring at the screen, a new text box opens that's flashing. "What does this do?" I press it just as Reese says "Wait!"

A video box pops up. Reese ducks down in her seat as a hazy outline of a girl with long, sleek reddish-blond hair and pale skin appears in the frame. She narrows her brown eyes at me.

"H!" she barks. "Where have you been? I've been calling you for hours."

She looks vaguely familiar. Wait a minute. "Celia?"

"Yes, it's me," she says impatiently. "Is your phone buffering?"

"Say yes," Reese hisses.

"Uh, yes! All morning. Wi-Fi was down at home. Sorry. Hi! How are you?" I play with the friendship necklace around my neck so she can see it. I notice she has the same one on. We're truly best friends!

"I've been better. I really need you to answer when I call," she says, and sighs. "Sorry. I'm just so stressed."

"About the launch," I say, proud I know that detail. "And Fenway Park."

Celia rolls her eyes. "Who cares about that? I'm talking about our thing. Did you finish reading the contract?"

"The contract?" I squeak. What contract?

"Say yes!" Reese whispers again.

"Yes! All done," I lie.

Celia looks relieved. "Good. I knew you'd make whatever changes were necessary so we'd get a good deal. Once you've read it over, we can both sign. Now we just have to get through today and tomorrow and we'll be on her way." She smiles bright. "C and H forever!"

I put my hand on my heart, touched. She really does care about our friendship! Something must have changed since that night at her thirteenth birthday party. "C and H forever!" I cheer. "I'm so glad we're friends."

"Yes, yes," Celia says distractedly. "Go enjoy your final breakfast meeting with Blake. I'll see you at the office." The screen goes dark.

Reese sits up again. "What did Celia mean by your last breakfast meeting with Blake?"

"Before the big event," I guess. "She sounded stressed." I look at Reese. "Should I be stressed?" What if someone asks me for this proposal?

Reese shrugs. "I'm sure all the big stuff is done. It will be fine. Ooh!" The car rolls to a stop in front of a brownstone with a blue door with numbers on it reading "185." "We're here!"

I look out the window. Newbury Street is a funky area of Boston that I've always wanted to explore more. They have all these little art galleries, boutiques, and pop-up shops selling everything from skin care and candles to comics, and little eateries like a pizza place with the name Dirty Water Dough, which sounds weird but is so good. Ava, Zach, and I were looking forward to coming here on our overnight trip to Boston.

For a moment, my stomach swishes slightly as I think about where Ava and Zach are right now. If I'm friends with Celia, did she become friends with Ava and Zach too? But there's no time to ask Reese these things because the Uber door is opening on its own and Reese is dashing up to the door and knocking.

I step out of the car and *oof!* I trip forward, grabbing a parking meter to hold me upright. (Unfortunately, meters still exist in the future.) Reese looks back at me and frowns. "Sorry! It's these heels," I say. My feet wobble as I try to stand up straight again. These shoes have wedge bottoms and have to be at least two inches high. I loved how they looked in my closet (my walk-in closet!), but now that I've got them on, I have no clue how to walk in them.

"Come on!" Reese calls as the door opens and a man in a suit steps out holding a clipboard.

"Name?" he says as I walk slowly (very slowly) to the steps and hold on to the railing.

"Harper Lancaster," Reese says, sounding important. "For a meeting with Blake Riley."

"Password," he says, and Reese and I glance at each other.

"I . . . uh . . ." Think, Harper! What would the password for an exclusive restaurant be? "Postcard?" I try, and Reese sighs deeply.

The man blinks. "No."

A girl brushes past us and stops in front of the guy.

Her dark hair is pulled into a high ponytail, and she's wearing a silver dress that glitters. She sees me and does a double take. "Harper Lancaster?"

"Uh, yes," I say, surprised.

She pulls me into a hug. "I love your videos! The one you did with music award show makeup hacks changed my life!"

"That one is good," Reese admits. "It has over six million views."

Changed her life? I am beaming. People know my videos!

"It's where I got the idea for this body glitter," she says, showcasing her arms, which are rippling with muscles. "We need to take a picture! My friends aren't going to believe I met you unless I have proof."

"A picture with me?" Wow, wow, wow! This is so cool. "Okay."

She taps her ear, and a screen appears with a camera icon. She moves in close, we smile, and two seconds later, I see our picture pop up on her screen. The girl looks around. "Is Celia here too?"

"No, but I'm meeting Blake Riley inside—if I can remember the password."

The man purses his lips, looking annoyed.

"Blake Riley?" The girl's eyes widen. "I need a picture

with her too." She links arms with me. "They are with me and the password is 'robin's egg.'" The man has no choice but to let us in.

I grab Reese's arm, and then we're inside what looks like a regular apartment with lots of small rooms. Tables and couches are in every nook and corner. Everywhere I look I see someone vaguely famous according to Reese, who is naming people in my ear.

"I'll be by later for a picture," the girl tells me, heading off to meet friends at a couch in the front room.

"Harper!" I hear someone say.

And there is Blake Riley in the flesh. My favorite TikTok star is here! She's ten years older but just as pretty, waving to me in a cute blazer and jeans with booties (glad to know they're still in style). Her dark curly hair looks wet, like she just got out of the shower, and her face is bare except for swipes of lip gloss and mascara. The look works for her.

"There's Blake!" Reese's mouth forms a wide O.

I know my mouth is doing the same. Blake Friggin' Riley is HERE!

I grab her arm to hold myself steady and take tiny steps in my heels to get to the table, feeling like my heart is in my throat. I know Blake Riley! This doesn't feel real.

121

"Blake, hi! Good morning!" I giggle uncontrollably. It's Blake Riley! I was just watching her TikToks in the bathroom at Sugar Crazy, and now I'm here with her in person!

Blake pulls me in for a hug, and I smell a mixture of freesia and lavender. "Today's the day! Are you excited? I'm so excited!" She dances around, doing a move I recognize from one of her videos. Around the restaurant, people glance our way, smiling. Blake glances at Reese. "Is this your sister? You two look so much alike."

"Yes, this is Reese," I say. "She, uh . . . she really wanted to come to today's event." Truth!

"Hiiiiiiii," Reese says, sounding a tad nervous as she waves to my boss. (Boss!) "Harper said I could come with her today since I'm supposed to shadow someone in a career I admire for school." She winks at me.

Smooth. Why didn't I think of that?

"That's great." Blake beams and motions to the waiter, who brings over an extra chair and table setting. "We love helping tweens and teens get their start, don't we, Harper?" She touches my arm as we sit down. "That's how it happened with me and your sister. I found her videos online and thought, who is this twelve-year-old makeup genius?"

"Genius?" I touch my chin to force my mouth to close. I'm beaming.

"Yes, and you were sweet as sugar too," Blake says, and looks at Reese. "The two of us connected in messages, then collaborated on a Stitch video or two, and the rest is history." She sits back and looks at me. "That was a long time ago. Even before you teamed up with Celia for your C and H TikToks." She smiles. "But I always knew you were a star."

Me? A star?

Blake looks at Reese again. "I don't know how I'd run this place without my marketing gurus."

"Marketing gurus," I repeat, excited. "It sounds so adult."

Blake laughs. "Yeah, brand marketing, as I've quickly learned, is a lot of work," she explains to Reese. "I was a way better TikTok star than a businesswoman, but that's what I have your sister and Celia for—they know how to create the best image for the brand." Blake presses a button on the table, and a virtual screen pops up between us with a menu. "But enough small talk. I'm starving, and we've got a big day ahead of us! What are we ordering?"

Reese and I stare at the screen and stare at the

possibilities. Ooh, Nutella pancakes! Crepes! Ice cream for breakfast? I read off all the frozen coffee contraption possibilities. Doughnuts on coffee drinks. Ice cream cones IN coffee drinks. One made with edible chocolate-chip cookie dough (glad to see that's still a thing). There's even one called a Unicorn Surprise, with cotton candy topping and sprinkles. I'm not sure it's work appropriate, even if it sounds delicious. I see a group of teens at the next table ordered them because three drinks topped with cotton candy appear at their table. I'm practically drooling.

"What are you getting?" I ask Blake, unsure of my own decisions. I guess some things never change. She looks like a mint-cookie-dough-frozen-whipped kind of girl. As a matter of fact, I think she endorsed one once at a big coffee chain.

Blake taps the screen. "What I always get. A coffee, black with two sugars, and a fruit cup. I'm boring that way. You?"

I deflate. How grown-up of her. "I guess I'll get that too, then."

"Reese?" Blake asks.

"I'll take the Unicorn drink," she says. "And Nutella pancakes."

My stomach rumbles at the thought. That sounds delicious.

Blake taps the screen and adds our order to hers. "So," she starts. "How is everything looking for today? I saw your memo come in late last night with confirmations on Harry performing, the fireworks show after the event, and a few menu changes for the party. Why are you up at one a.m. on email?" She shakes her head. "You work too hard!"

"Wow, I do," I agree. One a.m. emails? "I guess there's just still so much to do for the event." Maybe if I keep saying the word "event," something will click.

"Who are you kidding? I knew you could handle this job from the moment we did the Your Lips Only Better line three years ago. You've got it all under control." Blake leans forward on the table. "But I did want to see you before we rev up for the event tonight. I'm going to be so busy today. I think the PR department has me doing at least a hundred interviews, podcasts, and streaming appearances just to get ready for it."

"That sounds like a lot," Reese comments.

"It is." Blake shrugs. "But if my name can help sell this green Face of Beauty line, it will be worth it. It's important to me that our products are clean, healthy, and ones you feel good about using. As an animal lover, I love that we are starting to use cruelty-free ingredients and this green line is a big deal. Want to see a picture of my number one guy?" she asks Reese.

"Yes!" Reese says, eating up Blake's every word, as I am.

Blake clicks her ear. A screen pops up with a picture of a bulldog.

"Aww, he's cute!" Reese gushes. "What's his name?"

"Ronald." Blake grins. "He's my world. I rescued him from a shelter three years ago, and we're pretty much soul mates." She turns back to me. "The idea of anyone testing products on animals of any kind just makes my heart ache. That's why this line is so close to my heart. I don't just want the face of green beauty to be another brand. I want it to be one you can trust is doing what it can for the environment, our bodies, and our animal friends. I want this line to work. I *need* it to work. We all do." Her face, free of blemishes, or any of the makeup she's selling, clouds over.

I frown. "Why wouldn't it?" I ask as our very bland-looking coffees are placed in front of us. "It sounds like exactly what the makeup world needs."

"And it is," Blake says, and catches Reese's eye.

"Work cone of silence, okay?" Reese nods. "I just can't help but worry when we launch something new."

"People love you!" I pick up my coffee and eye it suspiciously.

"But people also think I'm just a name attached to a brand and I don't know what I'm doing." She bites her lip. "I want them to see me as a smart business-woman who is going to be in this game a long time, but even I worry. When will this ride be over?" she says with a shrug. "At some point, some new, younger star will come along with a makeup line that is hotter than mine and attract double the amount of followers on some new app and I'll be forgotten. You can only stay on top for so long."

"You're going to be here forever! You're Blake Riley," Reese says, sounding completely at ease talking to an adult who is also a star. She oozes confidence I don't have. What gene did she get that I didn't?

I bring my lips up to the cup. Coffee even smells terrible! Meanwhile, Reese's Nutella pancakes and her Unicorn drink arrive, and I can't stop staring at them. Maybe my coffee won't be that bad. I take a sip.

"I appreciate that, but I'm thirty-two," Blake is say-ing. "How long can this fame game last?"

Thirty-two? I spit the scalding-hot coffee all over our table.

Blake jumps up and a waiter comes running over. "Are you okay? Is it too hot?"

It's like drinking mud! How do parents like this stuff? Reese looks mortified. My cheeks burn. "Yes, too hot," I lie. "Sorry."

"I'm so sorry." The waiter takes the offensive cup away. "Can I get you something else instead? Maybe something to cool down your tongue? The Unicorn drink is really popular."

I perk up and look at Blake. "I mean, if it will cool my tongue down, then I guess I could have something as juvenile as the Unicorn," I say stoically. But inside I'm thinking, YAY! This is a huge improvement. Reese tries not to laugh.

"One Unicorn," Blake tells the waiter. "Make it two. We are celebrating! Today is a big day." She winks at me. "And I couldn't do it without my star employee."

Blake loves me. Like truly loves me! "I won't let you down today," I vow.

"And I'm happy to help with whatever you need," Reese says.

Blake leans over and hugs her. "Well, then we'll have to thank you for interning with some form of payment.

128

Your sister can take you to the beauty closet, where you can stock up on anything and everything makeup-wise you need for free."

I pause as my Unicorn drink is placed in front of me. "What's a beauty closet?"

Blake and Reese burst out laughing.

"She didn't sleep much last night." Reese covers for me. "As if anyone could forget the famed beauty closet in all your TikToks."

I shrug and give a little laugh. "Exactly! Kidding!"

But seriously—what is a beauty closet? If it's free makeup, I want in immediately.

10

Blake has two more meetings after our breakfast one, so Reese and I say goodbye and take an Uber to the office, where our first stop is definitely going to be the beauty closet. I just hope it's easier to get into this building than it was One Eighty-Five.

"This place looks like my dermatologist's office," I say as Reese and I walk into the palatial lobby and approach the security area. "But it's much bigger."

There is a huge water fountain in the middle and photos of Blake that cover every wall. There're also a lot of pictures of a chunky bulldog that I assume is Ronald. People are coming and going, electronics are beeping, and the water feature is loud, but I still say hi to everyone I see. This is really exciting. I'm a co—marketing director! Whatever that means.

"Good morning," I say to the security guard at the

first stop. "How's your day going?" He just looks at me. "It's nice out, right? Bring your umbrella with you, though, if you go outside between one and two, because it's supposed to rain." The security guy looks at the guard next to him. "Hi!" I say to him as well. "How is your morning?" He recoils slightly. Strange. "This is my sister, Reese. Can she have a pass to come up?"

"Whatever you want, Miss Lancaster," the second guy says, handing the pass over and stepping away from me. "Sorry about making you wait the other day. It won't happen again."

"No problem," I say, noticing as he goes to an intercom on his desk and whispers something into it. The first guard waves us over to an open elevator, which whisks Reese and me upstairs.

As the doors open, I hear someone shout, "She's here!" I can hear chairs scraping, and then I see a woman come racing toward me.

"Harper, hi. Good morning," she says, stammering slightly. "We weren't expecting you for another half hour. Otherwise, I would have had your coffee order waiting for you, but I swear, I can have it here in five minutes."

I blink taking in her frizzy, thick brown curls. I know her! *"Saya?"*

"Morning," she says, sounding nervous.

"You work here too?" Maybe all the Cambridge Street Girls work at Face of Beauty. I have a sudden image of Celia and I employing our entire friend squad. That has to include Ava and Zach. I wouldn't leave them behind.

She steps back. "I know I messed up that delivery at Fenway yesterday, but you did change it three times—not that it's ever your fault—but I promise everything you need today will go as planned. Just give me another chance." She whispers, "Please don't fire me from this internship. I need it for credit."

"Fire you?" I glance at Reese, unsure what is happening.

That's when I hear frantic barking.

A familiar-looking bulldog comes tearing toward the elevator doors.

"Ronald, right? Hi, buddy!" I exclaim. I put my hand out to pet the dog, and he starts to snarl. I press myself against the back wall in horror and look at Saya as I stand protectively in front of Reese. I wonder if I could offer one of these heels to eat instead of me.

Reese crouches behind me. "Wow, he really doesn't like you."

"Nope," Saya says a bit too quickly. "He's never

warmed to you or Celia, but I'm sure it's nothing personal."

"Why would it be personal?" I ask as Ronald continues to bark.

"It's not like you've thrown out any of his favorite squeaky toys or locked him in the conference room. Ronald, be nice to Harper," she adds, but not convincingly. If anything, she seems to be enjoying my discomfort.

Locked a dog in the conference room? I want to be a dog walker . . . or I *did* want to be a dog walker. I've never met a dog that didn't like me before.

Reese steps in front of me and offers the dog her hand to sniff so that he'll calm down. "Hi, Ronald!" Ronald sniffs it, then sits down and lets Reese pat his head. "Aww, he's a sweetie! Do you have any treats? That should win him over."

"Why would I have any treats?" I ask.

"You always have one in your bag to keep him from growling at you," Saya tells me.

"I do?" I reach into the bag I'm carrying—and sure enough, there's one of those dental chews that Milo likes. I toss it to the dog, who stops growling and grabs the treat, then saunters off like he owns the office, which apparently he does.

Saya shifts uncomfortably. "Problem solved! So do you have a coffee order for you and . . ." She looks at Reese expectedly.

"I'm her sister, Reese. And our first stop is the beauty closet. Can you show us where it is? Harper hasn't been to it in a while."

"Sure," Saya says, looking at me strangely. "Let's move before he turns on you again."

She walks past a reception desk with a huge Face of Beauty sign and into the office area. People keep their heads down, otherwise I'd say hello, but I do smile at everyone we pass. It's a large room with tons of cube seating and a few offices partitioned off with glass walls. People are working in clusters at a few large tables in the center of the room or having conversations on the phone—*I think*—while transparent TV screens hover in front of them as they talk. I can see someone watching what appears to be a photo shoot in front of the Eiffel Tower right from their desk here in Boston.

"Here you go." Saya clicks open a door and walks into what can only be described as paradise.

It's a large, windowed room with floor-to-ceiling shelves full of makeup and nothing but makeup! In one corner is a massive mirror in a gilded frame. A makeup table with remover pads and Q-tips sits at the ready, along with a pink tufted chair. The makeup on three walls says Face of Beauty, while the fourth wall contains rival brands' products.

"It's like our own personal Sephora!" I say breathlessly.

"Awesome." Reese races to the first shelf she sees.

"And we can really take anything we want?" I ask Saya.

"*You* can," Saya says, shifting awkwardly. "Celia has me on freebie probation, so . . ."

"What is freebie probation?" I ask as I spritz perfume into the air. It smells like rain. Love!

"For what happened with the Fenway delivery." Saya sounds miserable. "If you guys hadn't changed the order three times, I—"

"Oh, that's silly!" I cut in. "Take what you want. Blake said it's all extras." Saya just stands there, looking alarmed, so I drag her over to a bookcase and point to some lip liners. "Go on! You said you're interning? You deserve it."

Saya gapes. "Wow, that's really nice of you."

How can I not be nice? It's like I've won the lotto. Every piece of makeup is staring back at me from clear cubes and trays just waiting to be applied. Multiple versions of every type of lipstick, lip cream, lip gloss, and lip tint I've ever wanted to try is right here for the taking. There are also eyeliners, face scrubs, mascaras, and eye masks. I slowly walk over to the first shelf and marvel at the dozens of tubes just waiting to be used. I lift a pretty pale pink lip stain off the shelf and stare at it lovingly. Reese already has her arms full. Saya quickly gets her a Face of Beauty bag, and Reese throws stuff inside it. Saya does the same. She's about to drop a face primer into her bag when I see her pause. Someone has just rushed into the room.

"There you are!"

"Celia!" I throw my arms around her. She's gotten very tall and is wearing sky-high heels and a fitted pantsuit. Her reddish hair is pulled back into a sleek ponytail, and she's wearing dangling earrings that match our friendship necklace.

"I was just in the beauty closet helping Saya and Reese pick out some things. For free," I add. Still can't believe that part.

"Saya?" Celia wrinkles her nose. "You're still here?"

"Heading on a coffee run for Harper." Saya thrusts her bag at Reese and turns to Celia. "I'll get your usual. I have to get for everyone at the meeting, so it might take me a while to carry all the trays."

"I can help you," Reese offers, and looks at me. "You don't need me right now, do you?"

"No." I shake my head, feeling more settled now that I see Celia here and she seems happy to see me. "Come find me when you're back."

Celia shoots their retreating backs a look. "I want my coffee with cinnamon spice. Not pumpkin pie spice. Get it right this time, Saya!" I hear the door close behind them. "I've been looking for you everywhere! And I thought you fired Saya yesterday," Celia says pointedly.

"Fired? Me?" I blanche. I can't even speak up at the cafeteria when the lunch lady gives me the wrong side with my pizza. (I don't do applesauce.) How could I fire someone? "Aren't you friends with Saya? She's a Cambridge Street Girl, no?"

"Was," Celia says, picking up a brow brush and twirling it in her fingers. "Now she gets us coffee and is an intern toiling away in boring grad school classes."

"Why do I have to fire her? She said she fixed the delivery thing with Fenway Park."

"Because I asked. What's up with you anyway?" Celia opens the door to the beauty closet, and motions for me to follow her into the hall. I clutch my bag to my chest and run behind her.

"I didn't sleep well," I try. "Because I was up so late doing emails."

Celia smiles. "And our contract? When can I sign it?"

The contract again! What is this about? "Soon," I promise. "I meant to email it to you after we talked, but it's been so hectic with the event." I wish I knew exactly what I was doing at this event.

Celia's expression is guarded. "We have a lot of money riding on this. You know that we—"

Ronald is back and the sound of barking is so loud than I can't hear the rest of what she's saying. Ronald has clearly finished his treat and is now ready to bite our legs or my bare toes.

"I hate that dog! Ugh! That slobbering mess. Why does Blake like that thing?" Celia laments as she hops up on someone's cube desk to get away. "Do something, H!"

Geez, I don't remember Celia being this bossy.

I rumble around my bag looking for another treat to fend off Ronald. There's none. Hmm . . . what to do? Looking around, I spot a small stuffed duck sitting on a computer in the cube Celia is hiding in. I grab it. "Ronald, want to fetch?" I say in my gooiest baby-ish voice—just like I always talk to Milo. Ronald stops barking when he sees the duck. It doesn't squeak, but it does look like a dog toy. "Ready, Ron?" I hold it high over my head and throw it down the hall. "Go get it!" I shout, and Ronald takes off after the duck.

Celia jumps off the desk and goes running down the hall, leaving me in the dust as Ronald comes tearing back our way. I flinch as he nears, but he just drops the toy at my feet and wags his stump. I guess he's warming up to me.

"Want me to throw it again?" I toss the duck, and Ron runs after it a second time, then obediently brings it back without a snarl or a bark. The two of us are getting into a groove of catch and release in the quiet office, the sound of the air-filtering system the only noise other than murmurs from the conference room. I hear a door down the hall open on Ron's fifth throw.

"H! My office! Let's go!" Celia calls to me, waving me down the hall.

"Coming!" I yell, pulling off my heels and running down the hall barefoot.

"Hellish Harper is on the move!"

I turn around, hearing my name, but everyone is bent over their desks, working. Did I just hear someone call me Hellish Harper?

"H!" Celia yells again.

"Coming!" I slide into the office and shut the door behind me before Ronald can come back. Celia clearly doesn't like him. I turn around. "What a view!"

The office has a giant floor-to-ceiling window that

139

looks out onto the city of Boston. I can see Fenway Park from this window and the Prudential Center.

"You have one just like it," Celia says as she locks the door behind her.

"I do?" I look back at her. "I mean, I *do*!" I laugh nervously and walk around the office, glancing at framed photos. Me and Celia in middle school with what looks like the Cambridge Street Girls . . . on their actual block! Celia and me with Blake at an event. Celia and me at a ribbon-cutting ceremony with Blake, looking older. Celia and me with Blake and Taylor Swift on a giant float in turquoise-blue water. Next to that is an award made out of glass. I read the inscription: *TikTok Influencer of the Year: Celia Darrow and Harper Lancaster*.

WOWZA. I pick up the award and put it back down. "We've done everything together, haven't we?"

Celia sits down in her swivel chair and looks at the award on the spotless black desk. "Yeah, we have. And that's why it works. Like we said in the original proposal you wrote for investors, we have that influencer magic." Her smile fades. "I can't wait to get through today and just move on already. Tomorrow is going to be our day."

"Right." I'm trying hard to follow. "The proposal."

"Yes!" Celia flashes me a grin. She comes around

the desk and squeezes my hand. "It's finally happening. I can't wait to tell the world."

"Me too." I pause. "About . . . ?"

Celia laughs. "Our deal! We're so close to signing and then all this"—she waves her hand, her pale pink manicure gleaming in the florescent lighting—"will be peanuts compared to what we'll be making."

"We're getting a raise?" I guess.

Celia's eyes glitter. "A big one. Just send me that contract, okay? I want to do my digital signature before the event tonight so we can have everything in place. Then we're out of here."

I get a strange feeling in my stomach. "Out of here?"

"I don't want to face Blake." Celia shivers. "Our makeup packaging is almost exactly the same as hers. She is going to flip, but there is nothing she can really do about it. We've checked all the loopholes. She can't come after us. She never paid enough attention to her own brand to know how to safeguard against this sort of thing."

"We're doing our own makeup line?" My mouth feels chalky. Now all Celia's questions about the "contract" make sense. We're leaving Blake and she doesn't know it. Thinking about the Blake I met at breakfast, my heart gives a lurch. Blake is so nice and has clearly done a lot for us. Why would we do that to her?

Celia rolls her eyes and swats my arm. "H! You're too funny! Now come on, we need to do a video." She taps her ear, and a screen appears. "Let's do the dance from that new Erika song."

"Erika?" Who's that? Uh-oh. "I haven't learned all those moves yet. Can we do something else?"

"Nope!" Celia taps the air, and the video screen mirrors us. "Smile! But no teeth! Just copy me!" The song starts, a thumping bass and lots of yelling disguised as singing filling the air. Whoever Erika is, I'm not a fan.

Celia is doing these complicated arm movements to the beat that remind me of a clucking chicken. I catch her glaring and attempt to sway in place instead. I don't want to look like a chicken.

"This is C and H," Celia says into the camera. "Catch you on the flip side!" Celia presses the screen. "And done! Let's play it back."

Eek. We look ridiculous. "Should we reshoot that?" I ask pleasantly. "It's not that good."

"Who cares." Celia swipes screen away. "It will go viral anyway. Everything we do does."

But we look silly, I want to say, but looking at Celia, I can't. What if she disagrees or gets mad at me? *So what?* a small voice says, but I shove it aside.

"Now we just need a caption." A text box appears on the translucent screen. "'Meeting with my bestie to come up with your new favorite new Face of Beauty lip sheen shade. What do you want to see next?' End!" Celia shouts, and the text fills in. She swipes the screen again with her finger, and it disappears. "We need to make sure we repost that to all of our social accounts. Oh! And we should get some pictures of all of us at the Fenway walk-through with the new lip sheen on the table. It's the perfect final Blake post before we go out on our own with a better one."

"About that," I start to say, but before I can try to talk to Celia, a new screen appears in front of me. "Harper?" I see my grandma's right eye appear in the screen. "Harper, is that you? Can you hear me?"

"Grandma?" I say excitedly. She looks great! "Hi!"

Celia swipes Grandma away.

"Hey! That's my grandma!" I protest.

"This is no time for distractions, H," Celia says. "The last thing we want is to fizzle out like Blake Riley." She nudges me to the door. "You have a contract to send me so we can finalize things. I can't believe you brought Reese with you today of all days."

"I know, but she wanted to come to the event," I say quickly. "She said she's never met Blake."

"That's because you hate spending time with your sister."

"I do?" The chalky taste in my mouth is back. I don't understand why I wouldn't want to be around Reese. She seems really cool.

"Just keep her out of our business. We don't need any leaks." Celia looks down at my feet. "And you have to get rid of those shoes before the walk-through at Fenway. They're terrible."

"They are uncomfortable," I admit.

"Use the expense account and SkyMail new ones to your office," Celia suggests.

"Expense account?" I repeat.

"Might as well use it a few more times before we give it up. I will miss that perk." Celia sighs. "But not the lousy paychecks. Blake has never paid us enough." She winks. "But no need to worry about that anymore. We're the bosses now!"

Bosses? I hear my stomach rumble. "Listen, about the contract, maybe we should talk about this some more."

Celia squeezes me tight. "We're done talking. Now it's time for action." She pulls out of the embrace and looks at me. "We are doing what we've always wanted to do—rise before Blake drags us down. Tomorrow is going to be the best day ever!"

11

• • •

I don't know what to do with myself after that con-versation with Celia. All I know is the idea of double-crossing Blake Riley makes me feel ill. Why would twenty-two-year-old me do such a thing? Now I'm contemplating what just happened by twirling around in a purple chair in my office (which is identical to Celia's down to the pictures in the frames). Suddenly the door opens and Reese breezes in with a tray of iced coffees.

"Hi!" she says happily. "I got you the same vanilla bean drink I got because you didn't seem too hot on the coffee at One Eighty-Five this morning. I got us some chocolate chocolate-chip cookies too. And get this: Saya paid for everything on a corporate card. She said it's all charged to the company. Free coffee!

Seriously, you have the best job ever." Reese sees my face and freezes. "What's wrong?"

"Can you help me read my emails?" I blurt out. "Or my documents using my earphone thing?" I tap my ear, and the clear screen pops up. "I need to find a contract."

"Sure. Do you know what it's called?" Reese puts down the tray and coffees and offers me my vanilla milkshake coffee drink.

I shake my head. My stomach is a mess after talking to Celia. "I don't, but I'm sure it says 'contract' in the title."

Reese begins swiping through screens. "Well, you have over two hundred contracts on here. Any way to narrow it down?"

Great. I lean over and look at the screen, trying to think. I must find this thing! "Something about a new makeup line contract?"

"Um . . . oh! Wait! This contract was last opened yesterday, and it's in a folder marked 'private.'" Reese clicks on it, and a Word document appears on the screen.

The two of us stare at the title: "C&H's Face of You, an investment opportunity with Jameston Cosmetics International." My stomach churns even more.

"C and H's Face of You?" Reese repeats. "That sounds like a rip-off of Face of Beauty." She glares at me. "Are you and Celia starting your own company?"

"It looks that way." My heart is beating fast. Reese gives me a nasty look. "I don't remember doing any of this," I protest. "I don't even remember being twenty-two before this morning! Can you stop pouting and just search for a proposal with this C and H's Face of You in the title?"

Reese types a few more things and a new screen comes up. "Here you go."

I scan the document and see my name all over it. I can tell Reese is reading everything too. It's a proposal for the C&H Face of You model. There are a lot of numbers on the page I don't understand and talk about valuation, and TikTok milestones, plus stuff about Celia's and my rise to fame, plus talk about how the C&H makeup line will appeal to a younger demographic than Blake's. I think I'm going to be physically ill. We're starting a rival makeup company behind Blake's back!

I keep clicking through the pages and see a bunch of designs for makeup packaging. They're so similar to the Face of Beauty boxes, it's scary. Even the makeup product titles are similar to Blake's. So is the company title! What's worse: the proposal talks a lot about how Blake's star is waning while Celia's and my numbers on TikTok keep rising. To capitalize on that, C&H's plan is to launch all the products on TikTok and do special promotions and pricing to undercut Blake's bottom line. Basically, if we keep our pricing lower than Blake's, we claim our products will be an easier sell.

Reese groans. "Tell me this isn't true! You guys are going to claim your products are green and cruelty-free without paying to certify they actually are?" She motions to a line in the document about how some companies pay for a rabbit icon to appear on their packaging to prove their stuff is cruelty-free. This proposal says you wouldn't pay for that step. "And you're going to use all the same manufacturers for your products that Blake does to deceive consumers?"

"Why would we do this to Blake?" My voice is shaky.

"Maybe because you're a horrible person?" Reese narrows her eyes at me. "You wrote this proposal, you signed this contract. All that's left is for Celia to sign too. You're stealing Blake's company and making it your own! Harper, how could you?"

Reese is right. Twenty-two-year-old me is a horrible person. "I don't understand any of this. Blake is the whole reason anyone knows us on social media. She gave Celia and me these jobs." I think back to breakfast. All that talk about helping rising stars. And now we're turning on her? "I can't believe we would do this to her."

Reese folds her arms across her chest. "I can. When we were getting coffee, Saya said something to me about how awful you and Celia are to everyone at work, but I didn't believe it. Now I'm not so sure."

I sink lower in my chair, wanting to disappear. "Awful?" Maybe that's what Saya was talking about when she said she was afraid I was going to cancel her internship. "I'm not awful . . . am I?"

Ding! A private message pops up on the screen in front of us. "For your eyes only," it says, and it's from Celia. Reese opens it, and we both read what it says.

Did like you said and called several of our contacts and told them not to bother coming to the launch tonight. Talked to Harry's people again and I think Harry is going to be a no-show for the performance. Blake is toast.

Oh no. Oh no. Oh no. Oh no! Why would she do that? The text is followed by three laughing-face emojis. I start to hyperventilate.

Ping! Another private message pops up, also from Celia.

Can't believe you thought of this! You're brilliant! How great would it be if no one shows up? Attached invite list so you can reach people and tell them to just wait for our product launch announcement party next week instead. Blake will DIE when she sees we've taken the new eco-packaging idea and made it our own! We'll get Harry to perform there instead. C&H RULE!

I close the message and sit back in my chair, stunned. Reese and I are quiet for a moment, the air-conditioning whirring in the office the only sound between us. Outside in the hall, I hear Ronald barking and people talking, but in here, it's like a tomb. What has Future Me done?

"It's official: I am a horrible person," I whisper.

"Yep," Reese agrees. "You're the worst."

"How did this happen?" I wonder aloud.

Reese shrugs. "You think I know? You don't talk to me about anything."

I think back to Celia's comment about how I can't stand my only sister and I feel even worse. "We're not close?"

"Close?" Reese snorts. "I see you more on TikTok than I do in person. You're never home. You barely talk to Mom and Dad, and you never talk to me. Most of the time when I do see you, Celia is dragging you off somewhere with the Cambridge Street Girls." She rolls her eyes. "You do whatever she tells you to do."

Like steal my boss's ideas? I feel bile rising in my throat. I've never been good at speaking up. I guess that hasn't changed in the last ten years. "I don't know what to do here," I admit. I can feel tears spring to my eyes.

Reese leans over and hugs me. "You'll figure it out."

"How?" I wonder aloud.

Reese steps back and looks at me. "Whenever I don't know what to do, I think WWTD."

"WWTD?" I ask.

"What would Taylor do?" Reese says, her cheeks

reddening slightly. "As in Taylor Swift." I just look at her. "That's one thing we've both always had in common—a love of Ms. Swift."

"True," I agree.

"And Taylor always knows what to do," Reese insists. "Think of all the songs she's written. Every one of them is about experiences she's had with friends, boys, school; both the good and the bad. She figures things out because even when life gets hard, those experiences make you who you are, right?"

What would Taylor do? I wonder. She'd probably go to her friends for advice. Could I go to Taylor? We did vacation together, but the truth is, I don't remember that and I don't know Taylor. I don't even know Celia all that well. Who I really need is my best friend. *Ava.*

"I have to find Ava!" I announce.

Reese frowns. "Who is Ava? Wait. I think I've heard Mom mention her name before. Was she your friend in middle school?"

"Yes," I say, sounding shrill. Looking around my office, I don't see a single picture of her or Zach. "She was my best friend! But she never liked Celia. Ava didn't even want to go to her thirteenth birthday party with me, but I made her come."

Reese raises her right eyebrow. "Is that the one

where you made this so-called half-birthday wish on TikTok?" I nod. "Well, I guess that answers your question. If Ava wasn't a Cambridge Street Girl, and you only hung out with them, I guess you guys stopped being friends too."

Stopped being friends. That sounds so permanent. No. It's not possible. Ava and I wouldn't have just gone separate ways. I rack my brain trying to remember something—*anything*—from the last ten years, but I can't think of a thing. How could I have let this happen? Ava is the best person I know. She always has the best advice, whether it's about dealing with my parents or putting pink tips in my hair. *Ava would know what to do here,* I realize. I need to find her. I stand up and look at Reese.

"I need to see Ava. Any clue where she is?"

Reese shrugs. "Not a clue. But we can probably find her on social media." Reese pulls up her own screen. "Got her! She graduated University of Massachusetts Amherst with a degree in veterinary sciences and now she's taking a year off before going for her doctorate at Tufts University. Sounds like she's still in Boston."

"Ava always knew what she wanted to do," I say, a tad enviously. I never had a clue what I wanted, but Ava always wanted to be a vet. It makes me wonder if she ever got that dog-walking business off the ground. "Can you figure out where she is right now?"

Reese narrows her eyes at the screen and swipes some more. "According to this latest post, she's working at a vet clinic near Northeastern University. Oh, and it looks like she lives with friends that go there. Hang on." She swipes past three more screens, and I see pictures fly by. "Yep, her roommates are girls who go to Northeastern like Saya," she says triumphantly.

"You got all that from her posts?" I say, surprised.

Reese nods. "It's all on here. The only thing I don't see is an address, but Alice can get you one." She leans over to tap my ear, and I shrink back.

"Do not stick your finger in my ear. I'll do it myself if I have to." I click my ear with a groan. "I hate these new phones."

"Really? I've seen pictures of old phones, and they're massive," Reese says. "Who wants to carry a heavy thing in your pocket?"

"I wish I had it now," I lament. "Alice?" I ask my phone. "I need an address for an Ava Peña in Boston. Can you find it for me?"

"Sure thing!" Alice says immediately. "Ava Peña lives at 4025 Parker Street. She is in unit 215 on the second floor." A map pops up on a screen along with a tiny figure walking. It's just a few blocks from here. "Shall I initiate walking sequence guide?"

"Alice, you are the best!" I say. "Thank you."

"You're welcome. Thank *you*, Harper. This is the first time you've ever said that to me."

Reese just shakes her head.

My face warms. "I never say thank you?"

"Once. But I think you were saying it to the sushi delivery guy. I accepted the praise anyway."

I swallow hard. Alice appears to do everything for me. I can't believe I've never thanked her for that. Well, that's about to change. "Then thank you for all the times I didn't say it and should have." I look at Reese. "Got the address. Can you cover for me while I go find Ava?"

"*Now?*" Reese says incredulously. "You have a walk-through at one p.m. at Fenway for an event you're trying to tank *and* you're trying to destroy Blake's company. Don't you have more important things to take care of?"

Yes, I think. *Ava can help me figure out how to fix things. I'm sure of it.* I grab my bag and head to the door. "You said you wanted to intern, then intern!"

"What does that even mean?" Reese asks.

I open the closet in my office and look at a row of shoes. Ooh, flip-flops! Score! I pull off the uncomfortable wedge heels and slip into a pair of green flip-flops with—wait, are those plastic codfish on them? No matter. They're flip-flops. I'll take them. "You're going to help me do some damage control. Go into my email and find the invite list. Then call everyone on it and tell them the party *is* on and they need to come tonight."

"And if that doesn't work?" Reese asks.

I shrug. "You're my sister," I say. "I'm sure you'll think of something." I go to the door. "I'll meet you back here after my Fenway meeting so we can get ready for the event together. But call me before then if you learn anything important."

"Okay, and what are you going to do?" Reese demands.

I take a deep breath. "I'm going to find Ava and try to get my old life back."

12

• • •

Ava can get me out of this mess.

Out of the two of us, she's always the one with a plan. It doesn't matter what we're talking about—a social studies test on Greek mythology, whether jean joggers are a good or bad idea, or if I need an extra swig of mouthwash after eating a garlic knot—Ava gives it to me straight. She is the best person to have on your side in a crisis because she always offers a solution. And yes, sometimes that can be annoying when I just want to gripe, but in the end, I know I have to figure things out eventually. So why not take her advice?

I just hope she's willing to give me some today.

Ava's apartment is near the Northeastern University campus, which, according to Alice, isn't far from the office. Instead of hopping in an Uber, I walk, taking in the sights as I go. Boston looks exactly as I remember it. Tall buildings are nestled between tiny historic places, and signs pointing to the Freedom Trail walking tour, Paul Revere's house, and Faneuil Hall are everywhere. Many people are walking too, which is a relief (I was worried we all had flying cars in the future), and the tiny cars Reese and I took this morning to get to One Eighty-Five are super quiet as they zip down the street. After a few blocks, my phone tells me to make a left, and I see Northeastern's campus up ahead. I can see a lot of students standing around the grassy knoll playing hacky sack or sitting on the ground talking. Near them are a bunch of tents, and I can hear live music playing. The T (which is the name for Boston's subway system) pulls to a stop by the campus, and I watch people hop off, chatting about getting food and meeting up after class.

"Ooh! B-Cappella is playing!" I hear a girl say as she brushes past me. "I love them. Do we have time to watch?"

"I wanted to go to the fair," says another girl. "Can we do both?"

"Sure, but let's hit the fair first," the first girl says. "We don't want to miss the freebies."

Oooh, freebies? Like as in Sephora freebies? I love the ones you get for shopping there all the time. And

I love samples. I'm sure twenty-two-year-old me likes samples too. The girls link arms and I can't help but stare at their retreating figures. Ava and I were like that once. Ava is probably still like that. It makes me wonder what she was like in college. Future Me never went, according to Reese. I went from my GED to working for Blake, and yes, I know school didn't come as easily to me as it did Ava, but seeing all these people on campus makes me wonder suddenly what it would be like to go here.

What would Taylor do? I think. I don't know what a B-Cappella is, or this fair, but it's only ten-forty-five on a gorgeous spring day and I've never been on a college campus before. Taylor would check out this college fair. I follow the girls into the quad and immediately I know I've made the right decision.

Northeastern's quad is in party mode. An a cappella group is performing on a stage while a second group waits offstage with instruments to go on next. People are gathered on blankets on the lawn or are standing to watch the performance. They're cheering as if this group is . . . well, whoever we're supposed to be into these days.

To the left of the stage is a row of tents with signs touting clubs to join on campus, like a cappella, photography, crew, and even a dental club (which is handing out free toothbrushes and dental floss). I walk closer. The recycling club is giving away reusable bags and collapsible water bottles to anyone who will sign a petition to keep the Charles River clean. Next to their tent is the cooking club. I approach the table and listen to the speech the girl behind the table is making about the benefit of making your own protein bites from scratch.

"Are you interested in joining the Well-Seasoned Chef?" a girl asks me. She's wearing a Well-Seasoned Chef apron, so I guess that's the club name. She holds out a tray of what looks like lemon squares.

"I am," I say, taking a square and stuffing it in my mouth. Wow, it tastes like pure butter. Yum. "What do you guys do?"

"We get together once a week to bake treats to sell at the sporting events or cook a meal for one of the food shelters in the city—" She stops short. "Hey, are you Harper Lancaster from TikTok?"

"Yes," I say with my mouth full. "Hi."

"Your tutorial on eyebrow shaping changed my life," the girl gushes. "Have another square."

Who am I to argue?

"Do you go to Northeastern?" she asks.

Oh. "I . . . I'm really interested in learning how to bake," I say, skirting the question. It isn't a lie. As I watch the girl next to her knead dough by hand while a third person powders a fresh tray of lemon squares, I'm intrigued. Baking looks sort of peaceful. No wonder Reese wants to run her own food truck. I hear my phone start to ping and click ignore on my ear.

"Great!" The girl smiles at me. "Sign up here with your dorm number and cell, and we'll get in touch with you for your first meeting." She passes me a clipboard.

I stare at it. I don't have a dorm room. No matter. I do have a cell. I'll just put that down and a random dorm room number. No one will check, will they? Maybe I can actually go to a meeting. I picture myself in an apron and one of those cute baker's hats with flour all over my nose. I wonder what they're baking next. Maybe I can suggest hojarascas, which are Mexican shortbread cookies Ava and her mom always made for the restaurant. I could make some and bring them to her apartment. I hand back the clipboard.

"See you at the meeting," I say, rushing off to the dental booth to grab some floss and a toothbrush. Then I stop by a digital club booth to learn about making movies. I'm not sure I'm into that idea, but I do like the next booth, Northern Promoters.

"We do local college events' promotion and marketing," explains the college student behind the table, who is also handing out highlighters. I love a good highlighter! "Hey . . . did anyone tell you that you look a lot like Harper Lancaster?"

I take a green highlighter from his hand and smile sweetly. "I get that a lot."

"Cool," he says before going on to tell me about how the club promotes event nights and most recently did a game night.

Zach, Ava, and I did game/movie nights all the time. Our favorite game was Trouble, and it makes me wonder if Trouble still exists in the future. I was always the best at rolling a six and getting my little peg figure out on the board. *Zach* . . . I think of his half-birthday gift and my stomach starts to swish. Where is he right now? Is he still friends with Ava? I need to get going and find out.

"What dorm are you in?" he asks.

"Dorm East," I say quickly, seeing a sign right out of his line of vision that says EAST CAMPUS THIS WAY. There must be a Dorm East, then, right?

"I've never heard of that one," he says.

"We're very selective." My phone starts to ping again. "There's a wait list."

He nods. "I've been wait-listed for Parker for six months."

"Hopefully you'll get in soon," I tell him. I click the ignore call button again on my phone. Who knew college had so many clubs or activities? Mom's mentioned them about the college she works at, but I guess I never really paid attention. She always told me when I got to middle and high school there'd be all these new opportunities. I guess she was right, but jumping from twelve to twenty-two, I've missed out on everything. Suddenly, I'm sad.

I hear a dog bark and jump. The next tent over has a pen full of puppies. *Ava!* I think. Could it be that easy—could she be working this booth right now? I wander over and read the sign on the booth: "Helping Hands with Animals." Sadly, there is no sign of Ava.

"Hi there!" says a girl at the booth. "Are you interested in volunteering at a no-kill shelter for puppies?"

Ava volunteered for one of those. At a no-kill shelter pets are kept on-site until they're adopted and can't be euthanized.

"Ours is amazing—we even have a vet practice on-site—but it's expensive to run, so we volunteer as many hours as we can and fundraise for food and other animal needs." She cocks her head to one side. "You're not Harper Lancaster, are you?"

Wow, I can't believe my TikTok is this popular! It's cool being recognized but also kind of unnerving. What if I say or do the wrong thing and someone videos it? I put my fingers to my lips and wink. "Trying to keep a low profile, but I'd love some info on your shelter." I sign my name and write my cell number down, wondering if Ava knows this shelter.

I turn to leave and come face to face with a guy with a stack of flyers. "Friday pop-up party on the quad. Wear school colors! Hope you can make it!"

I take a flyer and read it over fast—free food, live music . . . This too sounds fun, but it's during the day, and I have a grown-up job. Future Me has a job. *Or did have a job*, I think darkly of Celia and my plan. I need to find Ava fast.

"Hey," I say to the guy. "Do you know where Parker Street is?"

"Hang a right at the end of the quad. It's the next block."

"Thanks!" I hurry off again. My phone is pinging, but I keep walking and finally see number 215 on

Parker Street. It's a high-rise building like mine. Someone is exiting as I approach, so I grab the door and slip inside. The similarities between our buildings end there.

Instead of a doorman and a stark, empty lobby, the main floor is bustling, and that's not a bad thing. There's a huge lounge with TVs, vending machines, tables, and students studying together. Banners announce upcoming campus events and club activities. There's one about a drive-in movie night on the Charles River and a group whale-watching trip around Boston Harbor. Someone sails a Frisbee past my head, and I duck to avoid getting hit.

"Sorry!" a guy yells before jumping over a couch and flinging the Frisbee back to a boy across the room.

A group of people screech as the Frisbee sails over their heads, barely missing a study group at a large table. Spotting the elevator, I head straight toward it, but I can't stop watching the students. Why does everyone look so happy at school? Doing homework?

School has never come easy for me the way it does for Ava or Zach. I have to study for hours to break a B on a test, and even then, it's after much coaching from Ava or Zach when we review stuff together. At the end, I usually just say, "Yeah, I get it now," even when I don't. Admitting that I don't understand our math homework makes me feel dumb. And I hate feeling dumb. But no one here seems to be trying to make anyone feel bad.

The elevator doors open on the second floor, and I make my way to her apartment. I can hear music and laughter the moment I near the door.

"Left! That's the way we slide! Slide! Slide!" someone croons off-key and immediately I know it's Ava. She's tone-deaf. She won't even sing in the car with me! And yet, I can hear her clear as day belting out lyrics to a song I don't know.

The song ends, and I hear a chorus of "Yeah, Ava!" and cheering. I go to knock and the door opens with my fist inches from it. A girl with bright blue hair sees my fist and ducks.

"Whoa! Almost caught me there!" she says cheerfully, as if almost getting hit in the face is a normal occurrence. "Are you here with the cookies? What do we owe you?"

I blink. "Cookies?"

"Yeah." She reaches in her pocket and pulls out what looks like a credit card. "The ones the drone lost in that bird strike?" She shakes her head. "That's the second snack delivery we've lost because of pigeons this week. This is why I still prefer human delivery people, but they're so rare now." She smiles. "So what do I owe you?"

"Oh, I . . ." I look behind the blue-haired girl and see a bright, airy living room where several girls are dancing around. "I don't have your cookies. I'm actually here to see Ava Peña." I swallow hard. "Is she here?"

"Yeah." The girl opens the door wider. "Come on in. AVA! It's for you!"

"Okay!" I hear Ava shout.

"I'm heading to class, guys," the girl says. "Catch you later. Mac and cheese for dinner?"

"With lobster?" says another girl, and everyone laughs.

"We can't afford lobster. We're doing mac and cheese in a box, but fancy!"

"Yes!" says a girl with her hair in a high bun who is sitting on the edge of a worn couch. "We'll set the table!"

The girl with blue hair winks at me and walks out the door.

Now I want mac and cheese. And I want to eat it

with these girls and be here when their cookie delivery shows up. If another bird strike hasn't ruined it.

"Are you from housing about the new roommate share?" adds a girl in the kitchen.

"Umm . . . no." I look down at my flip-flops and dress again. I guess, compared to these girls in leggings and sweats (glad they still exist too), I look like a grown-up. Suddenly, I'm not sure I like the feeling. "I'm just here to talk to Ava."

"Ava! Get your butt out here!" the girl shouts.

My legs are shaking as I step farther inside the apartment. The smell of Italian cooking mixes with the scent of a candle lit on the crowded kitchen counter. The living room is full of mismatched furniture and colorful rugs. Inside one bedroom off the living room I see unmade twin bunk beds, where a girl is watching a movie on a transparent screen.

In the living room, several girls are swiping at a different transparent screen as they debate what song to sing next ("No, not Bieber! He's ancient now!"). A girl with long black hair notices me and does a double take.

Ava.

She's older, of course, and she's grown about four inches, but this is definitely my Ava. She's just as petite as I remember, and her hair is exactly the same—pin-straight and long, reaching the center of her back, which always looked good on her. She's wearing jeans and a cartoon T-shirt.

"Harper?" she gasps.

"Hi! Hey! Hi!" I say, my voice shaking more than I'd like. "It's really you!" I can't believe how nervous I am.

The music cuts out, and everyone looks at me. Ava is quiet. "What are you doing here?"

What would Taylor do? She'd be honest. She'd start at the beginning, I'm sure, so that's what I do. I take a deep breath and try not to feel embarrassed. "I'm hoping you can tell me what happened at Celia's birthday party."

13

"Do you mean Celia Darrow's birthday party?" Ava looks from her roommates to me as she plays with a strand of her long hair. I nod. "That was like . . . nine years ago."

"Ten," I correct her, "but it feels like yesterday."

Actually it feels like today because it was today, but no use trying to explain all this. "You look exactly the same, though. Just taller." Everyone is so much taller! Ava doesn't say anything. "I just have a few questions. It will only take a minute." My sentences are coming out in chunks, and I feel warm and uncomfortable. I clutch my new recyclable bag with the toothbrush and flyers. "Please?"

"Wait. Are you Harper Lancaster?" one of the girls asks before Ava can answer me. "Ava, you didn't tell us you know C and H!"

"Actually it's more like I 'knew' H," Ava says, looking away.

My stomach gives a lurch. *Knew.*

Ava looks at me again and I see a familiar furrow of her brow. "Are you wearing codfish flip-flops?"

"Yes." I smile brightly at her roommates, who stare at my feet. "So can we talk? I don't have a lot of time."

"Sure," Ava says, and motions to some sliding glass doors. "We can speak out there."

I walk past the girls, smiling awkwardly again, and I hear one whisper, "'This is C and H, signing off! Catch you on the flip side!'" The other girls start to giggle.

Our TikTok catchphrase really is awful. I hope I wasn't the one to come up with it.

Ava's balcony has a view of the quad of North-eastern. I can still hear music from the quad not that far away.

"I don't really have a lot of time either," Ava says. "I have to be at work in an hour. So . . . what's up?"

It's taking all my willpower not to reach over and hug her. It's Ava! My Ava! My best friend in the entire world. The one who knows me better than anyone, who is always pushing me to be more, do more. "It's so good to see you. Like really good! It doesn't feel like it's been so long, but I know it has been long, but it feels short. . . . Is it hot out here? I feel like I'm sweating."

Ava blinks. "Are you all right?"

"Yes," I insist. "Great. I'm twenty-two, just like I wanted!" I bounce on my toes, my flip-flops making a smacking noise against the cement. "Everything is perfect!" *Except it's not if I'm trying to steal Blake's company and I don't know how to fix things.*

Ava leans against the railing, watching me. "Great . . . so you said something about Celia's party?"

"Yes," I exhale before I start babbling again. "I was just thinking about it—you know, because it's been ten years, and I was telling Reese—that's my sister, who is now twelve and a half, by the way—about Celia's party at Sugar Crazy. The last thing I remember is getting up from the table and going to the bathroom."

"The bathroom?" Ava repeats, her brow furrowing even further.

How do I put this into words sounding like I lost my mind? "I was telling Reese I don't remember why we stopped hanging out after that night." I swallow hard waiting for her to say something. Somewhere in the distance at the fair, I hear an air horn.

Ava just stares at me. "You don't remember?"

"It's a blur. I feel like one minute I was in the bathroom, and you were knocking on the door and the next . . . bang! You weren't in my life anymore."

Ava hangs on to the railing. "We really don't have to rehash this. Like you said, this is all ten years ago. It's in the past. We've in our twenties now."

"Twenty-two to be exact," I say. "Your birthday is June twenty-eighth, so you're practically twenty-three." We both smile a bit at the fact I remember her birthday. How could I forget it? I was already thinking about what Zach and I were going to get her for her thirteenth. We were planning to track down some vintage Hawkgirl comics.

"Exactly," Ava says, her smile fading. "I'm over it. I'll admit, you dropping me like that hurt at the time, but we're not in middle school anymore. Thank god."

"Thank god," I agree. Just the thought of going back to that night, Celia's party, is awful, but so is not knowing who I was the last ten years. How did I become someone who would steal Blake Riley's makeup company? "So our friendship ended when I came out of the bathroom?" I try again.

Ava shrugs. "Basically. You finally opened the door and walked right by me and went back to the party.

You didn't want to talk to me. You just said you didn't need a ride home because you were sleeping at Celia's. After that, you didn't talk to me anymore."

If that's true, Ava doesn't know any more about my life than I do. How can I expect her to help me try to fix this thing with Celia and Blake if she knows nothing about me? This isn't like that time I misread a Halloween party invitation and Ava and I had ten minutes to revamp my costume. (I thought the invite said "Dress like a villain" when it really said "Dress like you're chillin.' " Ava and I turned my Evil Queen costume into the Snow Queen.)

With a sinking feeling, I realize Ava can't help me now. This Blake and Celia issue isn't her problem. It's mine. She knows nothing about Future Me's world. I've got to figure out how to fix things on my own. But what I can do is apologize for what a jerk I was. "For what it's worth, I'm sorry."

"Thank you." Ava and I stand there awkwardly for a moment before she motions to me. "But look at you! You're so successful now. I see you all over TikTok with Blake Riley. Remember how much you idolized her when we were in seventh grade? And now you work for her. Is she great? She seems so nice."

"She is," I say, and feel bad about what I've done all over again. "Really nice."

"And you're friends with all these celebrities, like Taylor Swift. We always loved Taylor and now you go on vacation with her." She shakes her head in awe. "Good for you, Harper. You got exactly what you wanted."

Exactly what I wanted. "Did you?" I wonder. "I heard you're studying to be a vet and someone said you work at a clinic near here. I can't believe you've known what you've wanted to do since we were twelve."

Ava nods. "I'm working at Helping Hands. Have you heard of them? They have a club on campus too."

"I met them at the fair. I was just passing through and stopped when I saw the dogs," I add hastily so she doesn't wonder what I was doing there. "They had the cutest puppies."

Ava genuinely smiles. "I know. I think they brought Freddie and Knox to the fair today. They're Chihuahua mixes, and they're the sweetest things. I really hope they get adopted soon. They've been in the shelter six months now. So many dogs and cats at the shelter need homes." She frowns again. "We're a no-kill shelter, so they can stay as long as they need to, but it would be great to find them families so we can take in more pets. There are so many out there that need help."

Like Milo did. Ava saw him and knew he was meant to be mine. It was Ava who helped me convince my parents I could take care of a dog. I've never been able to speak up like she could. My heart aches. Ava and I were good friends, and it is clearly my fault we're not even acquaintances. I hear my phone start to ping, and I quickly tap my ear, hoping it shuts the phone off. "I'm happy for you," I say, even though the thought of Ava doing these things without me also makes me sad. I guess I didn't do the dog-walking business with her. Did Zach? I want to ask her if they're still friends, but I feel weird bringing him up. "You're going to be a veterinarian."

Ava pushes a loose strand of black hair behind her ear. "I still have a lot of school ahead of me, but I don't mind. My roommates—they're the ones you met inside—all were undergrad at UMass like me and now they're going here, so I'm staying with them till I start at Tufts in the fall. I'll still get to work at the clinic too. It's a lot of fun, all of us being together."

"That does sound fun," I realize. I think of them making mac and cheese and doing karaoke and then see myself alone in my big apartment. Does it get lonely? Having only Alice to talk to? Not seeing Mom and Dad or Reese often because I work so much and am always traveling? I can't even fall asleep at night till I hear Mom and Dad in their room with the TV playing faintly. How do I live by myself?

"Well, I should get ready for work," Ava says, heading back to the doors. "It was nice to see you, Harper."

I freeze. So that's it? We're never going to see each other again? My heart beats faster. I don't think I can handle that. Maybe coming to see Ava was a dead end, but I can't imagine her not being part of my life anymore. "I should get your number so I can send you some Face of Beauty products. We have a beauty closet where I get free stuff," I explain. "And all the products are green."

"I know." Ava looks embarrassed. "I actually use Blake's stuff."

"Then I'll send you more!" I exclaim. "Just give me your number, and you can text me whatever mascara and shadows you use."

"Thanks." Ava plucks her phone off her ear. She holds it out to me.

I stare at it. Why is she giving me her phone?

"Oh." Ava pulls her hand back. "Do you not have your phone on you? I thought we could sync up and exchange numbers."

Sync up? I take my phone off my ear and hold it out to her, hoping I know what I'm doing. Ava clinks earpieces with me, and I hear a ding. Wow, that's pretty cool. My phone starts to ping again in my hand. I go to click it off, and a screen pops up. Celia's face fills the space between me and Ava.

"H? Where are you?" Celia demands. "The walkthrough is in twenty minutes, and you still haven't sent me that contract. I just want to sign it already. Are you on your way?"

Twenty minutes? "Getting in an Uber," I say awkwardly.

"Make it quick! I want to sign before we go into the meeting so everything is tied up!" The screen goes dark.

I look at Ava. "Sorry. That was . . ."

"I could tell," she says awkwardly. "Guess she hasn't changed."

"Yeah, well . . ." I shuffle to the door and slip inside the apartment. All of Ava's roommates have left, so it's just us. I want to fix things with her, but there is no way I can do that in the next five minutes. "Thanks again." Ava waves and I close the door behind me.

Then I RUN.

"Alice?" I call into my ear. "I need an Uber on Parker Street by Northeastern University right away."

"Hello, Harper. That will be no problem. One will be arriving in . . . two minutes. But while I have you, Reese has been trying to reach you. She says it's urgent."

"Tell her I'll call her after my meeting." I hit the elevator button and press it over and over till it finally comes. Thank goodness elevators work the same in the future. By the time I get out and make it outside, I see the Uber idling out front. I dive in and am thankful we zip through the city, arriving on Lansdowne Street by Fenway Park in ten minutes. I jump out and press my earpiece again.

"Alice? Any clue where my meeting is in Fenway Park?" I look up at the ballpark, which is clearly closed since there is no game tonight and we have an event. I try one entrance and find it locked, then run to the next entrance. "I'm not sure how to get inside. HELLO!" I yell through the gates, hoping someone can hear me. "ANYONE? I'm here for a meeting! I'm with Face of Beauty!" Still no one.

I hear talking and decide a whistle is in order. Dad taught me how to whistle when I was Reese's age—Reese the Wrecker's age, I should say—and I'm really good at it. I put two fingers in my mouth and blow. The sound echoes through the gates and the stadium. Finally, I hear footsteps.

"Hi! Over here!" I take off my flip-flop and smack the codfish embellishments across the gates. "I'm going to be late! Can you let me in?"

A figure emerges from the shadows. "Hi there. This is a service entrance. People usually have to go around. Who are you with?" the guy asks.

"Face of Beauty? I'm running the event that's happening here tonight. My name is Harper Lancaster." I wave a flip-flop in the air.

The guy looks at me. "Did you say Harper Lancaster?"

"Yes. Hi!" Another TikTok fan, probably.

He unlocks the gate and holds it open, stepping into the sunlight.

That's when I get a good look at his dark curly hair, tan skin, and killer smile. I drop my flip-flop. "You—you're my Zach!" I stammer. "What are you doing at Fenway Park?"

14

My face colors. "I didn't mean *my* Zach. I just meant a Zach I know." I stare at him some more. "You're so . . . muscley now." He laughs and my face warms more, but it's true. His arms are bulging out of the navy-blue Red Sox polo shirt he's wearing with jeans.

"Yeah, I started working out in high school. I was tired of being super skinny and having a mother always trying to fatten me up with Indian food."

"You look great," I say before I can stop myself. Wow, he grew up to be even cuter than he was in middle school. I'm completely tongue-tied as he reaches down and offers me my lost flip-flop.

"Codfish?" he questions. "I thought you hated fish."

"I did. I mean I *do*," I correct myself, and slip my shoe back on. "These were in my office and I didn't want to wear heels, so I grabbed them since I was running late."

"Better than putting together a Snow Queen costume last minute," he says with a wink.

"Not everyone can go as the Stay Puft Marshmallow Man," I say, thinking back to Zach's *Ghostbusters* costume, which wasn't exactly "chillin'" either. He may have looked like a snowman, but he was a marshmallow.

"You and Ava teased me about that forever." He runs a hand through his hair and continues to stare at me. "I can't believe it's you."

"And I can't believe it's you!" I exclaim, the two of us grinning like idiots. It's Zach! My Zach! The same Zach who never tagged me when we played at recess in third grade. I always got a free pass, which drove Ana insane, but I loved it. I've liked him forever and now he's standing right here in front of me. I sigh, happy just to stare at Zach's face. Then I remember he's standing right in front of me. I quickly look away. "So what are you doing here? Do you work for the Red Sox?"

He nods. "I'm part of the travel management team. I help organize all the guys' travel. The team is on the road the next few days, which is why you're able to have your event here."

Zach works for the Red Sox! "I can't believe you got

a job with your favorite team! You were always quoting baseball stats at lunch while you ate your Takis."

He laughs. "Sadly, I had to stop eating Takis— they burned my tongue—but I did get a job with the team. I interned here in college and . . ." He shakes his head. "Enough about me. Look at you, Ms. Fancy Tik-Tok Star. Looks like your life turned out the way you wanted as well."

"Did it?" I wonder aloud. I was obsessed with having a TikTok account for sure, and I tried to be like Blake, but Zach and Ava always knew what they wanted. I never did. Is working for Blake something I wanted, or did it just happen? I wish I knew.

"I remember your first TikTok post—it was for Taylor Swift's '22' video," he says, "and for your birthday I gave you that Olivia Rodrigo scarf and sunglasses to do her 'Déjà Vu' video." He looks embarrassed. "But you probably don't remember that."

I remember! I remember! "Not true. I loved that scarf. I thought it was so sweet that you bought me a second half-birthday gift."

"You probably don't know this, but I had the biggest crush on you back then," he says.

My whole body tenses. Zach *liked me* liked me too? "You did?" I whisper. "Why didn't you tell me?"

He shrugs. "You started hanging out with Celia Darrow's Cambridge Street Girls and I just didn't think I fit the mold of guys that your group dated."

Internally I'm screaming. "I would have gone out with you," I blurt out, my heart racing.

We just stare at each other. Finally Zach speaks.

"I guess I should have asked you out then," he says with a shy smile.

For a second, I wonder if he's going to ask me out now.

"I'm really glad I ran into you today. I was going to track down your email or call your office."

I feel a sliver of hope. "Really?"

"Really. I'm not sure if you do this sort of thing, but I help out with a mentoring program through the organization and one of the girls in my charge really looks up to Blake Riley. She says she's going to work for her someday."

I try not to feel disappointed. What Zach's doing is amazing, and of course. He tutored younger kids in middle school and was part of every philanthropic club the school ran. But a small part of me thought he was going to ask me out. "That's great."

"I'd love to ask Blake to write her a note of encouragement," Zach says. "Do you think she'd ever do that?"

"Definitely," I say, because knowing what little I know about Blake, I suspect she would. "I'll ask her. Just send me the kid's name. Is your cell number the same?"

"Yes." He grins. "Thanks, Harper."

I hear my phone ping again and remember I still have a crisis with Blake I need to solve. "By any chance do you know where the walk-through for the Face of Beauty event is?"

"Yeah, they're doing it in the courtyard area," Zach says. "I'll take you over there." He shakes his head again. "I can't believe it's you."

"And I can't believe it's you," I say, feeling giddy. I can't stop staring at him. "Are you coming to the event tonight?"

"I don't have an invite," he says, "but it sounds like some party. Harry Styles is playing, right? Or was." He frowns. "I heard someone say he just canceled. I saw Blake on my way over here, and she seemed really upset."

Oh no. Am I too late to fix this? "I'm sure we'll work it out." *I'll get him back,* I think as my heart lands in my throat.

WWTD? Taylor would take charge and that's what I'm going to do. Reese is calling people and telling them to come as we speak. I'm sure I can convince Harry to come back too even if Celia told him not to. I just need time to fix things.

"You always do," Zach says.

"H?"

I turn and see Celia walking swiftly toward us. "There you are! I've been calling you over and over. Did you forget to charge your phone?"

I don't even know *how* to charge my phone.

Celia grins at Zach. "Hi. Celia Darrow."

"Yeah, I know," Zach says. "We went to school together. Zach Kaur."

"Oh!" Celia says, recognition dawning on her face. "I guess you do sort of look familiar." She turns her back to him and focuses on me. "We really have to go." She puts her arm around me and steers me away. "Bye, Zane."

"It's Zach," I say, looking back at Zach, who just smirks as if to say, *Classic Celia,* and I'm realizing now it probably is. "You don't remember him?" I whisper.

"Ummm . . . vaguely? Wasn't he that weird guy who did the sports announcing for the baseball games?"

I stop short. "He isn't weird. He's smart and funny and cute," I say woefully. And he liked me.

Celia pulls me into an alcove next to a concession stand for bacon on a stick. "H, what is going on with you today? You're acting weird. Even for you."

"Ouch." *Even for you?*

"You know what I mean! This whole hyper, 'I'm so nice and I like Blake now and I just want to have fun and bring my sister to work' thing isn't going to work at our new company," Celia says flatly. "We got here by being taking what we wanted and not worrying who got stepped on along the way. That's how you stay on top. And now, suddenly, you've stopped listening to me and taking my calls twenty-four/seven? And you *still* haven't emailed me our contract to sign?" She glares at me. "Do not tell me you're getting cold feet."

It dawns on me that this is my chance to talk Celia out of this. Even if she's staring menacingly at me and it's making me uncomfortable. I need to hold my ground. For once in my life, I have to speak up. I take a deep breath. "You're right. I am off today. And you're also right that I'm getting cold feet. What are we doing, Celia? Stealing Blake's brand and doing a copycat one? Tanking her launch event? Why? Blake's been good to us and what we're doing is icky, sneaky, and just plain wrong."

For a moment Celia says nothing and I wonder: Have I gotten through to her?

I hear Celia exhale hard, and I choke on the scent of whatever mint gum she's chewing. "Who cares if it's icky? This is our chance! I'm sick of being in Blake's shadow. Jameston Cosmetics International wants to invest in us. Do you know how big that is for two girls who only know how to dance to TikTok videos and apply lip liner? I'm not giving up my shot to have my own company. Blake is yesterday's news! If we don't create our own brand now, we will have nothing."

"But it's not our brand," I insist. "We're copying Blake's line and trying to tear her down in the process."

"This was your idea." Celia's brown eyes flash darkly as her tone harshens. "Okay, it was my idea too, but we both wanted this. If you try to pull out now and go back to Blake, I will tell everyone what you've done and say it was all your idea."

A chill runs down my back, but that could be the wind whipping through Fenway. "You wouldn't."

"I would. Look, I like Blake, but we've got no endorsement deals coming in like she had at our age. No film or TV offers. When you were creating new TikTok content for us left and right, we were doing great, but now that we're with Blake, we're only gaining three hundred followers a week. It's not enough. You were right—copying her beauty line and remaking it as our own is our only shot at staying famous. It's not like we went to college and learned how to do anything else."

I feel a tingle at the base of my neck. *Staying famous.* Is that what all this is about? Not doing the right thing, or working at a job I assumed we loved?

When I was twelve and a half, my biggest worries were impressing Celia and the Cambridge Street Girls, trying to gain followers on TikTok, and making Mom and Dad see me as an adult. Now I'm twenty-two and my problems haven't gone away, they've just become more grown-up. Twenty-two-year-old me doesn't see her family, doesn't hang out with her sister, lost touch with her best friends, and is trying to destroy her mentor's company.

How did I get here? Are all adult problems this confusing? This is way worse than facing the Cambridge Street Girls again and having everyone at school learn I wasn't actually invited to Celia's birthday party. I'm twenty-two, and if today is an indication of who I am, I don't think I like the Future Me very much.

Celia reaches out and squeezes my hand. "H, you know you want this. You just have cold feet. Sign the contract and send it to me and we can start our lives."

That's exactly it. I finally see things clearly. I don't want this life. How could such a great wish go south so quickly? That changes now. "I'm sorry, Celia. I'm not signing. I'm staying on with Blake."

For the first time since I entered the office this morning, I feel my stomach relax.

Celia stares at me. Her smile is sort of eerie as she clicks her ear and a screen pops up. She scrolls through messages quickly. "I see. I'll tell Jameson I'm going ahead on my own then." She types something fast and I hear a swoosh as the email disappears. "Maybe I'll have them announce my new company immediately. In fact, might be fun if the announcement showed up on social media right before the party. It's not like anyone is coming. Harry canceled; people are changing their RSVPs. You've helped tank Blake's company, and now you and the Face of You company are going to sink together."

Celia leaves me standing there listening to her heels echoing through the Fenway corridor.

As relieved as I am to have done the right thing, I also know I've royally messed things up for Blake and Face of Beauty. How am I going to fix this?

My phone keeps pinging, and I can only imagine who it is on the other end. Blake? Jameston Cosmetics International wondering why I'm pulling the deal? Someone else canceling on tonight's event? I lean against the nearest concession stand and consider drinking a vat of ketchup. Suddenly, I hear more footsteps and barking.

Ronald is barreling toward me, pulling someone

along behind him. For a moment I freeze thinking it's Blake. Instead I see Saya.

"Ronald! Slow down!" she yells, but Ronald won't stop till he reaches me. His nails catch on my dress hem and cause a pull.

"Ronald!" Saya pulls him down. "Oh, Harper, your dress! I'm so sorry."

"It's okay." I deserve it. I scratch Ronald behind the ears, and he sits on my toes, wagging his short tail happily. "Hey, buddy. Miss me?"

"He really seems to like you all of a sudden," Saya says, surprised. "I'm just glad he found you! Blake is over at the Bleacher Bar doing a walk-through, and it's a disaster. Harry Styles canceled! We have no performance! And I just spoke to people in the office, and they said people are calling and changing their RSVPs to no. Blake is looking for you everywhere." I hear a ping, and Saya touches her ear. If it's possible to look greener than she already does (standing in a very green part of Fenway), Saya does. "Nope. No. Can't be happening. Is this text right?" She looks at me. "Mara in the office just texted to say Celia's assistant got a text from Celia asking her to start cleaning out her office. Was she fired? Or did she quit?"

News travels fast. "She quit."

Saya's dark eyes widen. "Are you quitting on Blake too? Why is everyone quitting?" Saya grabs me by the shoulders in a panic. "I can't run this event alone tonight. I'm just an intern!"

Who knew Saya was so panicky? "Just breathe!" I breathe in and out slowly, trying to calm myself as much as I am Saya. She copies me, and we both continue our *shush-shush-shush* sound for a minute or two, a custodian staring at us strangely as he wheels a garbage can. "Better?" I ask.

"Yes." Saya swallows hard. "No. Maybe? I have to tell Blake about Celia. Mara said she doesn't think she knows yet." Saya holds up a tiny earpiece. "She had me hold on to her phone because it was pinging so much in the walk-through. I have to tell her." I yank her back.

"Don't," I say, panicked.

"Why not?" Saya demands. "Blake needs to know people have given notice. Why shouldn't I tell her?"

Ronald licks my leg and whines for attention. My phone keeps pinging. Everything is spiraling out of control, and I have no one to blame but myself. Or Future Me, to be precise. It's time to make things right.

"I can fix this," I swear.

Saya gives a little snort. "And how are you going to do that?"

"I'm not sure yet," I admit. "Let me think, which is hard to do over my phone constantly ringing." Time to face the music. I click my phone, and as the screen pops up, I wait for the screaming to start. "Hello?"

"HARPER!" Reese's face is pressed against the screen so that I only see one of her brown eyes and half her nose.

The second Saya sees who it is, she stops and stares at the screen. I've never been happier she's nosy.

"Where have you been?" Reese freaks out.

"Reese!" My stomach drops again with relief. "Sorry! I was busy. Are you okay? What's going on?"

"What's going on is I've been calling you for an hour and you don't pick up! Haven't you learned how to answer your phone yet?"

Saya's eyebrows raise comically. I guess she's not used to watching me get a tongue-lashing.

"I'm sorry." I rub my temples and feel a headache coming on. "There's a lot going on here! I'm in so much trouble. Celia is going ahead with the new company without me and—"

"New company?" Saya interrupts, but I ignore her.

"Harper, listen . . . ," Reese says, but I am on a roll.

"I saw Ava, but we're not friends anymore and I realized I couldn't bother her with this big mess when we don't even talk anymore, but then I ran into Zach and he said he had a crush on me in middle school and I should have told him how I feel, but I didn't and—"

"Harper!" Reese tries to cut in.

"Zach Kaur?" Saya interrupts again, looking around. "He's here?"

"Saya, please. I'm trying to properly panic here." I turn back to my conversation with Reese again. "And I don't know what to do and Blake is looking for me, Celia gave notice, and Harry is not coming, and I can't help thinking I shouldn't have made such a ridiculous wish. . . ." I close my eyes. "I didn't realize what I was asking. I just want to be twelve and a half again."

"What wish?" Saya says, and I look at her. I almost forgot she was standing here.

"HARPER!" Reese shouts in my ear, and I wince. "Stop talking! Listen to me. I've solved everything!"

"How?" I say, exasperated.

Reese grins. "I found your old phone. You can wish for your old life back!"

15

I've now added dognapping to my list of offenses today because, minutes later, I'm dragging Saya and Ronald with me into an Uber and racing back to the office to meet Reese, where she has my old phone. I couldn't have Saya blabbing to Blake about Celia, the party mishap, and all this wish business. If I wish myself back, none of this will have happened yet, and it *won't* happen. Problem solved!

"Where are you taking me? I have to bring Ronald to Blake!" Saya is complaining as I coax her into the car and Ronald happily jumps in beside her.

"Ronald will be happier in his dog bed at the office," I say as I cram in next to them and the Uber door closes. "Plus, I can't have you telling anyone what I just said or what Reese said till I wish myself away and fix things."

I know I'm not making sense, but soon it won't

matter. The second Reese said she had my old phone, I knew I had to get to it. Does it still work? Will the Tik-Tok app still have the birthday filter on it? Can I make a wish to be twelve and a half again? The questions are flying, and I don't know the answers to any of them. All I know is I have to get to my phone.

"Have you lost your mind? Wishes won't solve anything! They're not real!" Saya complains, pulling at her hair. "What is real is Blake freaking out that I've stolen her dog."

Yeah, that would be bad. I'd freak out if I couldn't find Milo. Ronald looks from me to Saya curiously, then licks my face. I think for a second about how to solve my first problem. "Okay, do this: Text Blake, and tell her you're bringing Ronald back to the office so she can get ready for tonight's event without distractions."

Saya crosses her arms and pouts. "Why should I help you? What have you ever done for me?"

"I didn't fire you this morning," I point out. "You said yourself: you need this internship credit. Why ruin things now?"

Saya sits up straighter. "Fine. Blake's probably coming back to the office after the meeting anyway. She has hair and makeup coming for an event that may not be happening."

"It's going to happen," I insist. The Uber makes a sharp right turn through the city streets. "But first, you need to text Blake!"

"Fine, sorry, jeez, you're so bossy," Saya grumbles as she pulls up a screen and sends the text. "Why did I ever take this internship?" she wails to the roof of the car. "I knew working with you and Celia was going to be trouble."

"We're that bad, huh?" I can't help but ask.

"No, I mean, I just kind of wish . . . It doesn't matter."

"No. What were you going to say?" I'm curious.

Saya sighs. "You wouldn't understand."

I turn to give her my full attention. "Try me."

Saya exhales. "Well, since you're talking about wishing, I kind of wish I had spent school going after what I wanted rather than what Celia wanted. And yet, here I am, interning at Celia's company to be near Celia when she makes my life hell." Her eyes look sad. "Did you know I wanted to join the science club at Havervill MS?"

"I didn't know you were into science." I'm flabbergasted.

"That's why I like the science of makeup," Saya says, perking up. "It's the only reason I wanted to intern here. But if I could do things differently, I think

I might have wanted to go into forensics." She looks wistfully out the car window. "Celia nearly failed earth science—her parents paid a fortune for a tutor—so she hated the idea of anyone doing science club. She made fun of it so much, I kind of forgot about it," Saya says. "I wish I had done it differently."

I wish. "You still can, you know," I say quietly. "It's not too late." I say it for myself as much as I do for her.

Saya thinks for a moment. "Maybe."

I listen to the sounds of the city. "While we're being honest with one another, you should know I want to do things differently too. If I can't wish my way out of this, I need to be a better person at work. Someone Blake and everyone else can rely on. I know I'm not well-liked there." Saya goes to protest. "It's okay. I heard someone call me 'Hellish Harper' this morning. I know the truth. You can tell me what a nightmare I've been."

Saya makes a face. "You can be pretty difficult. This week alone you sent me out to do your food shopping because you didn't trust a drone to buy the right brand of ketchup."

I wince. "I'm that particular about ketchup?"

"Apparently!" Saya turns to look at me. "And you're always threatening to fire people. You've got such a large ego because of TikTok. It's all you can ever talk about—your numbers, your fame, and who you're friends with." She rolls her eyes. "We're all so over it. Blake is down-to-earth. But you and Celia make everyone do your job for you, and then you guys take all the credit." She gulps. "No offense."

I hold my hand up. "It's okay. It sounds like I deserve it." I look at her curiously, wondering for a moment. "I thought since you and I were both Cambridge Street Girls, Celia would go easy on us."

Saya huffs. "You have a short memory. The CSGs fell apart once you became friends with Celia. Once she convinced you to stop posting videos on your own and do them with her, everything changed."

"Celia made me stop posting my own videos?" I say in surprise.

"Don't you remember? Yours were doing so well. Blake started commenting on them, and that's when Celia thought you should do a joint username and you listened to her." She rolls her eyes. "We all listened to her. No one has ever stood up to Celia."

"Speaking up for myself has never really been my strong point," I say grimly.

"Me neither," Saya laments. "It's hard with Celia. She takes credit for everything." She looks at me. "We all thought your videos were better than hers when you started out. She hated that, but it's true. I loved practicing how to apply makeup using your TikToks. I never told you that. I guess I was jealous."

"Of me?" I can't imagine Saya watching my TikToks. "I was always jealous of you and the CSGs," I admit. "Living on the same block, vacationing as a group. You and Celia did everything together. I wanted to be one of you to see what it was like to be popular."

"Sometimes I hated it. I wanted to move off our block," Saya tells me, looking worried. "Having to see Celia every time I walked out my door, and knowing we had to do everything together because our families were friends, was a lot sometimes. When Celia liked you, it felt like you were Blake Riley herself. But when Celia found someone else to orbit her sun, she cast quite a shadow. In a way, Celia was hanging out with you instead of me. I didn't have to do everything she wanted for a change."

Ava and Zach were never like that. Even if we were just biking somewhere to have lunch, the three of us had a vote.

"You took my place, I guess," Saya adds. "Then Celia convinced you to stop doing makeup tutorials and start talking about lipsticks and comparing brands, because she was hoping you'd reach creator status and start making money. I guess it worked, since you and Blake were already friendly online, but once you started hanging with influencers, you guys couldn't be bothered with anyone anymore."

I feel sad hearing that.

"I guess I'm not surprised she's leaving Blake," Saya says. "She always needs the spotlight for herself. Working for Blake was only going to last so long."

Saya is right. And for my supposed best friend, she was pretty quick to walk away when I wouldn't turn against Blake. Now she's left me holding the bag. I take a deep breath. "I'm sorry for being so awful to you now and back in high school. And for making you buy me ketchup."

Saya looks surprised. "Thanks. That's nice of you to say."

I shrug. "I used to be really nice. I guess I just forgot how to be."

Saya smiles. "At least you're trying now."

The Uber pulls up to the office and I put my hand on her arm. "So, listen. Could you please not say anything to anyone yet about Celia or Harry Styles? Even if Blake asks you?" Saya's face clouds over. "I just need fifteen minutes to try to formulate a plan," I beg. *Or make a wish.* "I have to find my sister first and talk to her, and then I'll include you in whatever those plans are. Please?"

Saya thinks for a moment. "I'm an intern. I'm happy to help when you ask nicely." She smirks and holds Ronald's leash tighter. He pulls to get closer to me. "You have fifteen minutes."

"Fair enough." I breath a sigh of temporary relief. "More soon!" I race ahead of her into the office, running past the Face of Beauty security and the staff. I don't stop running till I reach the safety of my office.

Reese is waiting for me.

She holds up my old phone triumphantly. "Problem solved!"

16

"My phone!" I cry, taking it from her and cradling it like a baby. It's just as I remember it from . . . uh . . . earlier today. It's got a cracked cover and everything, and the weight of it feels so good in my hands. I hate these new tiny AirPod-type phones. My old phone is way better. I look at Reese in wonder. "How did you get this?"

"When you left I started thinking of a way to fix all your problems, and I thought of your phone. I figured if you had it back, maybe you could make a new wish."

"I was thinking the same thing," I whisper. "We think alike." Reese grins. "But how do you have my phone from ten years ago?"

"Dad doesn't believe in adding to landfills, so he keeps all our old electronics that can't be recycled," Reese tells me. "I knew it had to be somewhere, so

I took an Uber home after you left—it was fine, I've taken Ubers by myself before—and I found your phone in the box of old electronics Dad keeps in the garage."

"I can't believe he still had it," I say, looking it over. It feels like I had it in my hands only hours ago. And that's because I did.

"I also found something else." She holds up a bracelet with jade beads and a small paw-print charm.

"That's the friendship bracelet Zach and Ava gave me on my half birthday this morning," I exclaim, slipping it on. My heart gives a lurch. I miss them both so much.

"The only thing I couldn't find was your phone charger," Reese says. "I tried a few chargers that were in the box, but none fit this model. I'm sure we can find one at a shop that sells vintage phones."

Vintage phones. As if my phone is from the early 1900s.

Reese pulls up a screen. "It looks like there is a shop on Comm Ave that fixes old electronics. It's called Tech-y Genius. I can run over and get a charger, and then you'll be in business." Reese smiles. "You can make another wish and poof out of here!"

Poof out of here. It all sounds so simple. If it's a dream. If this isn't my life. But what if this IS my life?

"Harper?" Reese waves the phone. "Why are you zoning out? We don't have a lot of time."

"What if I can't poof home again?" I ask softly. "Twenty-two-year-old me has really made a mess of things. I've helped destroy Blake's product launch when she trusted us with it, and now I'm going to try to leave her here to pick up the pieces."

"So what are you saying?" Reese asks. "You want to stay here after you've screwed everything up?"

"I'm saying, I don't want to just run out of here without making things right," I realize. "The whole reason I made a wish in the first place was to disappear after being embarrassed at Celia's birthday party. My answer is always to run rather than face things. I can't keep running."

"You're right," Reese agrees. "So what are you going to do?"

"I don't know." I sit down in my purple swivel chair and sigh. "I really thought twenty-two would be easier than twelve and a half. Taylor Swift made it sound so perfect."

"You mean in that old '22' song?" Reese cocks her head to one side.

Old. "Yes. The first TikTok post I ever did was

practicing the makeup in that video." I sigh. "Everyone looks so happy in '22.' They're hanging out at the beach and having the best time, and then they go to this epic party and dance without a care in the world. Twenty-two is when you're happy and free. There's breakfast at midnight! The chance of falling in love with strangers!"

Reese frowns. "Yeah, but you're forgetting the other part." Reese hums the song to herself. "Taylor also sings about being confused and lonely too, right? And how twenty-two is magical *and* miserable at the same time." Reese sits on the edge of my desk. "I love Taylor—WWTD and all—but I think she's saying twenty-two is just like any other age."

I look at her curiously. "What do you mean?"

"Every age is good and bad in some way, isn't it?" Reese asks, her legs swinging over the edge of my desk. "I like twelve because Priyaka and I get to ride our bikes all weekend and we have no plans, but I also have a curfew and need to ask Mom for money if we want to go get something to eat because I blow through my babysitting funds so quick. I'm sure twenty-two is fun for you because you have money and a job, but now you're always working and never have time to come home and see us or your friends, so that's not fun." She looks at me. "So I think Taylor is saying your age is what you make of it."

"I never thought of it that way before," I admit, and it makes me wonder what Taylor Swift would do if she was me, right here, right now.

She'd probably say she wouldn't trade any of her experiences because they made her who she is today.

When I made my wish, I didn't realize what skipping so much of my life would mean. I didn't get to experience high school or prom, or go on first dates (or date anyone—I see no sign that I've got a boyfriend), or figure out what could have happened with Zach. I have no idea if I would have convinced my parents to let me open a dog-walking business with Ava, or would have figured out what I wanted to do when I grew up. I'm a marketing director, but do I even know what a marketing director does? Do I want to work for Blake or a makeup company? Or am I here because of TikTok? I see now I missed a lot, including watching Reese grow into a very cool twelve-year-old I would be friends with.

I'm too stunned to speak. "When did Reese the Wrecker get so wise?"

She groans. "I always hated that nickname!"

"I'll stop using it—when I get back home," I say. "But first I need to fix twenty-two. And I'm going to start by telling the truth."

I think of Dad's favorite Mark Twain quote again: "If you tell the truth, you don't have to remember anything."

"I'm going to tell Blake what happened, and then I'm going to get people to come to this event tonight."

"Okay, but *how*?" Reese presses. "In case you've forgotten, your big draw—Harry Styles—is no longer performing. And I've been calling people on your guest list for the last hour and no one has called me back."

"What do people love as much as they love Harry Styles?" I wonder aloud. Harry Styles . . . he's cute, he's a good singer . . . he makes you feel warm and fuzzy inside. What else makes you feel warm and fuzzy inside? I hear a bark and sit up straight. "Dogs!"

"Dogs?" Reese repeats. "Dogs are going to make people come to a makeup launch?"

"Ava told me she works at a no-kill shelter near Northeastern and there are a lot of pets that need adopting. What if we bring puppies and cats to the event tonight? Blake said she wants people to know how green she is, and Fenway has a Green Monster wall, right?"

"*Right . . . ,*" Reese says, but she clearly doesn't get where I'm going with this.

"And part of having green beauty products is being cruelty-free and showing how much she loves animals, so if she brings puppies to Fenway and Face of Beauty helps people adopt, maybe we can get people to show up even without a performer coming. Everyone loves puppies!"

"They do love puppies," Reese says. "This could work!"

I start dancing around my desk, doing a routine that is clearly not made for TikTok. Reese does the same, then she stops and grabs my shoulders.

"Just remember, it's not me you have to convince; it's Blake, and you tried to destroy her company."

My heart gives a lurch. True. But one step at a time. "First step is seeing if Ava can get the puppies for the event tonight." I click my earpiece. "Call Ava Peña!" I yell, but nothing happens. I click my phone again.

Reese sighs and leans over, sticking her finger in my ear before I can stop her. "You've got to get better at this. Call Ava Peña," she says, and boom! A screen pops right up and starts dialing Ava's number.

The call connects, and I hear barking before Ava comes into the frame. She's holding a red tabby cat and wearing a pair of blue scrubs. She peers at the screen curiously. "Harper?"

"Hi! Yes! It's me!" I yell at the screen, then remember there is no need to shout. "I see you're at work. Great! I was wondering if you could help me with something."

"I'm kind of busy at the moment." The cat is trying to claw its way out of her arms.

"I'll be quick. I was wondering if you'd like to get some dogs and cats adopted at our Face of Beauty event at Fenway Park tonight."

Ava's face registers with surprise. "The one where Harry Styles is playing?"

Reese gives a little cough, and I wince.

"Um, maybe? We're still confirming his attendance, but either way it's going to be an amazing event, and maybe we can help some of your shelter pets find forever homes."

"At Fenway?" she repeats, sounding as skeptical as Reese did.

"My boss is a huge animal lover, and her new line of products is green and cruelty-free," I explain. "What better way to celebrate that than have a pop-up puppy and cat adoption on-site? I must clear things with Fenway, of course, but I'm thinking if we stick to Jersey Street and just handle the pet stuff outside the park, we can make it happen. We still have several hours before the event," I say, knowing even as I say the words out loud, it's going to be tight. But I can do this. *I must do this.* "We're expecting a hundred people at the event tonight," I say, looking at Reese for confirmation. She nods. "I bet many of them would love a pet. We'll be running things, so we could help you with adoptions."

Ava nods, thinking it over. "It does sound like a great opportunity. I'm not sure how we could transport them all there for tonight."

"We can help you," I think aloud. "We've got a large staff. We can help transport some pets." I hope.

Ava purses her lips. "Okay, Harry or no Harry, if we can get some of these guys adopted, I think it's a great idea. My manager at the shelter is always looking to help pets find good homes, so I'm going to go out on a limb and say this may work."

"Really?" I squeal. "YES!" I high-five Reese. "Go find Saya and tell her what I'm thinking," I tell my sister. "Maybe she can get some of the other interns and staff to start calling everyone on the RSVP list to tell them about the change in plans about the event and convince them to still come. And find out who we need to talk to at Fenway to get dedicated space to host puppy adoptions and . . . and . . ." My brain is working a mile a minute. What else would be fun to have at the event that works with makeup and puppies? "Maybe we can do puppy yoga?"

"Ooh, I like that," Reese says. "What else?"

I tap my fingers on the table as the barking at Ava's shelter continues. I have to keep it simple—small changes that involve puppies, but nothing huge since we're short on time. "We're already doing makeup tutorials, so why not conduct them with guests holding a puppy or cat on their lap? It's relaxing."

Reese grins. "I like that too. I bet you can even have someone here do a new graphic with the updated invite and put some pictures of puppies and cats on it."

"*Or*," I say, the ideas flying, "Ava, if you have any actual pictures of the pets that can be adopted, we can include links to them on your shelter site."

"That would be amazing," Ava says.

There's a knock at my door.

"Harper?"

It's Blake. Reese and I look at each other.

"Ava?" I say, feeling queasy. "I'll get this all firmed up and call you back with the details shortly."

"Sounds good," she says, "but hurry. We don't have a lot of time."

Believe me, I know. It's time to face the music.

17

When I open my office door, Blake has an entourage surrounding her. Some people are on their phones, some are taking notes, and one is even touching up Blake's makeup while she stares at me.

"You weren't at the walk-through," she says somewhat accusingly.

Here we go. "I did go to Fenway, but I had to leave quickly," I say as Reese skirts out of the room. I see her mouth "WWTD?" to me on her way out the door. My heart is starting to beat fast again. "I'm glad you're here. I really need to talk to you."

"I think that's a good idea." She smiles to the others. "Could you please give us a moment? Thank you so much." Her tone sharpens when she looks at me. "Harper? Follow me to my office."

My legs are shaking as I follow Blake into her much

larger office. Dozens of framed photos line the walls. Blake winning influencer awards, hanging out with celebrities, or posing at landmarks around the country with Ronald (Ron and her at the Grand Canyon! On Cape Cod! Driving in an RV!). Blake looks happy in every photo. But she's certainly not happy when she shuts the door and looks at me. "Do you want to tell me what's going on?"

Ping! I hear my phone go off. Thankfully, when I click it, I hear a voice in my head rather than see a screen pop up.

Reese

Saya and staff are on it. Calling all the RSVPs again. I'm running to find your charger!

"I just came from our company's launch event walk-through, where things seemed to be falling apart."

Blake's voice is eerily quiet, and I feel like she's my math teacher about to tell me I've failed the quarter. Or my parents questioning where I really was after school. (I said I was going for pizza, but really, we hung out on the playground at the park they think is sort of sketchy and should be avoided.) All I know, is her voice makes me feel uneasy. And when I'm uneasy, I don't speak up the way I know I should.

"When I tried to figure out what was going on, I found my marketing directors were MIA, so I couldn't get answers."

"I had to leave suddenly to take care of some details for the event," I say. Which is kind of true.

Blake's face is hard to read. "Then, on my way back to the offices, I got an email from Celia saying she'd quit. That came on the heels of Harry Styles's people attempting to cancel tonight's performance." She leans against her desk and looks at me.

Say something, the voice in my head says, but my back is to the wall and I'm panicking like I always do.

"Harry and I have been friends for years so I called him directly and you know what he told me? That someone named Celia called and tried to convince him not to do my event because her *launch* event with *you* was going to be even bigger."

My cheeks start to burn, and I'm sure I'm going to throw up on Blake's shoes. *Get it together, Harper! Tell her the truth! That's what Taylor would do!* My tongue feels chalky, and my palms are so sweaty, I fear if I try to hang on to the back of a chair, my fingers will slide right off. "I am not doing an event with Celia." There. I've said a single sentence. I can say another.

Blake raises an expertly penciled eyebrow. "That's not what I heard."

"Celia is going out on her own." My voice is shaking, but I keep going. Ron comes and sits on my feet, looking up at me happily. Spittle forms around his mouth and drips onto one of the codfish on my flip-flops. "She's starting her own makeup company, which is being announced today to take the attention off your launch and put it on hers. That's why she tried to get Harry to cancel." I swallow hard. "So he's still coming?"

"Yes!" Blake still sounds aggravated. "Harry wouldn't cancel on me. Who do you think creates his skin-care regimen? I'm the reason he still has a baby face."

"That's great news about Harry," I say. Especially the still-looking-young part. I'm sure Harry would love to pose with some cute cats and puppies for some promotional pictures. "I'll let everyone know he's still coming."

"That won't be necessary." Blake clicks her ear. A screen pops up, and I know instantly what I'm looking at—it's my rival makeup brand proposal. "You won't be at the event. You're fired."

My heart beats faster, and I feel like I might fall over. "Please, just let me explain."

"I've been in this business way longer than you have." Blake is eerily calm. "You didn't think someone would tell me that you and Celia were announcing a company that is an exact replica of mine? Or that you were trying to sabotage the launch event that I've poured my life into? The minute Celia started calling people about the event, I heard. I also learned about your rival company from those same people."

"No," I say, but she cuts me off.

"I didn't want to believe it was true, but I have proof on email. How could you?" Blake looks rattled. "I sat there and I talked to you about all my fears at breakfast, and you made them a reality. I thought we had a true partnership. When I found you on TikTok years ago and took you and Celia along for the ride with me, I never thought I'd see the day you'd turn on me."

I'm not sure I could feel any worse than I do at this moment. "Blake, I'm so sorry," I say, but the words feel empty. Even I don't understand what would make Future Me do this.

"It was always you I wanted to work with, you know," she says. "Your early TikToks were so clever. You weren't trying to sell products. You were just trying to be yourself and help people learn how to apply makeup. I loved them. But then you insisted your videos with Celia as C and H were even better, so I worked with her too." Her face hardens. "And now here you two are creating an identical company and ruining my launch." She turns away from me. "You should leave before I have security escort you out."

Ronald looks up at me, his paws still firmly planted on mine. Blake's telling me to go, and in a way, that would be easier. I wouldn't have to talk to Blake when she's this upset. I wouldn't have to apologize or even try to make things right. I could just disappear. But I don't want to chicken out like I've done a hundred times before. I want to help Blake fix this.

"I'm not leaving till you let me explain," I say, and Blake looks at me incredulously.

She points to the door. "Harper, I—"

"No." I cut her off, my voice stronger. "I'm not going till I tell you exactly what happened today and how we're going to fix tonight's event." She's quiet. "I just need five minutes of your time."

Blake stares at me. "You have four. Ronald? Come to Mommy."

Ron stays exactly where he is. I put my hand on his head and scratch behind his ears. "You're right—you trusted Celia and me as your marketing directors, and we tried to stab you in the back and steal your ideas." Whew! Glad that confession is out there, even if it's terrible. "But I couldn't go through with it. This afternoon, I told Celia I wasn't signing a contract with Jameston Cosmetics International. If she was going to create a rival brand, she was going to have to do it on her own."

"I'm glad to hear that," Blake says finally, "but you're the one who wrote that proposal for the rival company. Your voice is all over that document. You thought about double-crossing me and came *very* close to doing it. How am I supposed to trust you after that?"

"You're not," I surprise her by agreeing, "but I can't leave you with such a mess. I know you've been good to me. I don't want to see this event fail. I have a plan."

Blake gives me a look. "Forgive me, Harper, for not believing in your plan. I'm canceling the launch." Blake touches her earpiece to make a call, and I panic.

She can't cancel the event now! Twenty-two doesn't have to be a total bust! I need a chance to prove I can do something right. Heart pounding, I do the only thing I can think of—reach out and pull her phone off her ear.

"Harper!" Blake says, astonished. "Give that back!"

I hold it out of reach, then retreat into a far corner

of the room feeling a lot like Reese the Wrecker when she swipes my phone from me. Ronnie follows me, intrigued. "No! Not until you listen. I have a plan and I think it's a good one. Just let me explain." My phone pings again twice in a row. I click it, listening.

Reese

"We just got a call that the local news wants to cover the pet adoption tonight."

Saya

"Emails going crazy! Everyone loves the pet adoptions! People are agreeing to still come!"

"So you've gone from wanting to steal my company's ideas to wanting to save it?" Blake asks, sounding incredulous.

"Yes!" I say. "Everyone is doing green events these days. And yes, the Green Monster at Fenway is a cute play on 'green' things, but we can do more than just have Harry Styles sing at a beauty launch and talk about clean beauty. What does Harry even have to do with eyebrow serum?"

Blake folds her arms across her chest. Behind her, out the window, the sky is unbelievably blue with tiny puffy clouds. "Go on."

"You're an animal lover—you said so yourself this morning at breakfast," I start off. "Face of Beauty prides itself on being cruelty-free and not testing on animals. Instead of just focusing on how green the line is, why not take things one step further by supporting animal causes as well?" I look at Ronnie. "You rescued Ronald. What if we partnered up with a no-kill shelter in Boston to do animal adoptions at the event? And to bring the whole idea together, we could combine makeup tutorials at the event with animal meet-and-greets, adoptions, puppy yoga, and an animal play area. Harry can still sing, but while holding a dog and a cat. It's a cute visual. Then you could announce that you're going to give a portion of proceeds from this new line to your favorite cause—saving animals."

Blake sits on the edge of her desk, her long legs that I've seen dancing in so many videos still. "I like this idea a lot, but you won't be able to pull it off in a few hours."

"I will," I insist. "I already have the staff calling people and telling them the new idea, and we have press interested as well."

"So you said yes to this before getting my approval?" Blake asks.

"I was trying to fix things, and I think I've actually made them better. Or at least, I can if you let me," I say. "I can write something up for you to say."

Blake taps her fingers on her thighs. "So you're telling me you went from trying to steal my company to creating an entirely new event all in the last hour?"

I nod. "Yes. I know this doesn't make up for what I did, but I have to start somewhere. Puppies and makeup and puppy yoga felt like something everyone would like. I know I would."

Blake looks at Ronald, who finally trots over to her. "Puppies and makeup, huh? Why didn't you come up with this idea the first time around?"

"I guess I wasn't feeling like myself when we planned the event." *Truth.*

"Well, this is probably one of your best ideas ever," Blake says, and I beam. "We're going to go with it." She pulls up a screen and sends a text. "All hands on deck the next few hours. It sounds like you've already got things going, so I'm going to trust you know how to see this through."

"I do," I promise. "We won't let you down."

"And I am thankful you came clean about what was

going on here, Harper. I know that couldn't be easy to tell me the truth," Blake adds. "Since you've put it all together, I think you should be at the event to run it."

"Really?" I stand up straighter, feeling hopeful.

"But after tonight . . . I'm sorry." Blake looks at me. "You've betrayed me and this company. I still have to let you go."

My stomach drops again. "I understand."

I saw this coming, but still, seeing Blake's face, knowing what Future Me has screwed up . . . it's a lot to swallow. I've destroyed my whole future career, but I've made things right with Blake. I deserve what I get. All I can really control is tonight, so I'm going to give it my all.

My legs are shaking as I reach out to shake her hand. "Thank you for everything, Blake." I inhale sharply and attempt to behave like a twenty-two-year-old. I assume they wouldn't start bawling at work, so I won't either. But I do know one thing. "Next time I have a job like this," I promise, "I'll do better."

18

● ● ●

Maybe I am good at this marketing director business.

Standing back and watching the Face of Beauty launch event from the sidelines of Jersey Street, which we've taken over for the pet adoptions, I can't help being proud. (They'll all head into Fenway later to watch Harry perform and hear Blake's speech about the products, but the rest is happening outside the ballpark. There was no way Fenway was going to let all these pets roam their very expensive ballfield lawn.) Puppy yoga has been so popular it has a wait list, and puppies and makeup is such a huge hit, Face of Beauty's publicity department told me they want to try to make this a company staple at all events and do in-store makeup trials like this around the country with it too. I haven't bothered Blake at all—I'm trying to give her space—but she and Ronald are making the rounds and look pleased. It makes me feel good that I spoke up, owned what I did, and turned this event around.

"Fourteen applications for adoption already."

Ava is walking toward me, with Zach! I guess they're still friends. I try to remain calm. I didn't think I'd see him again.

"Hey . . . ," I say awkwardly. "That's great news!"

"We still have to do background checks, but if this goes through, we'll have cleared out a quarter of the pets we've had in the shelter for months." Ava's eyes are bright as she bounces on her toes, like she used to do when she talked about our potential dog-walking business. "And there are at least a dozen other people over there trying to sign up to see pets in the shelter or meet with the other animals we still have."

"Everyone seems to like the puppy yoga," Zach adds. I can't help noticing he's munching on a bag of salt and vinegar chips. "It made me even want to try yoga for a second."

Ava swats his arm. "Like you would ever try yoga!"

"Hey, I tried VR Twister for better posture," Zach says.

"VR Twister? That's a thing?" I don't see it.

"Wasn't for me." Zach sticks his hands in his pockets. "So I heard you completely revamped this event from when I saw you here this afternoon. That's impressive."

"It was nothing," I insist, even though I've been sweating through my dress for the last few hours trying to make sure it all came together. "This is the event we should have had all along. Thanks for coming."

"When Ava asked me to help her, I couldn't say no." Zach smiles at her. "She's pretty persuasive."

"It's not like you were doing anything but going home and eating Takis on your couch," she teases him.

"Hey, I told you, Takis burn my mouth," he says. "I've switched to salt-and-vinegar chips."

Ava and I look at each other. "Don't those still burn?" we ask simultaneously.

"Not as much," Zach insists.

"Well, thank you for skipping the chips-and-couch time and helping out with the event," I say, still unable to stop staring at him. He's changed out of his Red Sox polo shirt and is wearing a light blue tee and jeans. "I'm happy we get to do something good tonight rather than just give away free makeup." I look over at the large pet area, where people are meeting with puppies and kittens. There's a lot of barking going on, but no one seems to mind.

"Don't knock the free makeup," Zach says. "I promised my sister I'd get her a gift bag."

"You can bring her two," I say, and look at Ava. "You both can take as many as you want. I'm grateful for your help tonight. I know I don't really deserve it."

My best friend—the one who always sang Taylor Swift with me in the car, who hated mint chocolate-chip ice cream but liked mint ice cream, who I told all my secrets to (about Zach! Zach! Zach!), and planned my future with (okay, she planned and I sort of listened)—is not my friend anymore.

"I know I was a bad friend in seventh grade, and you both deserved better." I look at them again shyly. "If we're ever friends again, I promise not to take either of you for granted."

Zach and Ava look at each other, then back at me. "Thank you," Ava says awkwardly. "I guess I should go check on how adoptions are going."

"I'll see you over there," I say, still standing next to Zach.

"It was really good seeing you again, Harper," Zach says, his gray eyes landing on mine.

My stomach does a somersault at the thought of him leaving. They both sound so final. It's the kind of thing I've heard my mom say when she runs into someone she hasn't seen in a while at the grocery store and probably won't see again. Future Me is not a part of Zach's and Ava's lives anymore. This makes me feel sad all over again. Because what if Future Me is here to stay? I try to think of something that will make him keep talking to me.

"I had a crush on you in middle school too!" I blurt out.

He pushes his hair off his forehead and grins. "Did you, now?"

"Yes, but I was worried about what Ava would say about it messing up our friendship between all of us," I admit, my heart beating faster.

"I guess you and I should have told each other how we felt," Zach says.

I'm telling him now. Say it, I think. *Tell him.* The words are on the tip of my tongue as I stare at Zach's lips and wonder, not for the first time, what it would be like to kiss him.

But now he's going to walk away.

Potentially forever.

My heart is pounding. What would Taylor do?

Oh, what the heck.

I grab Zach by the back of the neck, pull him

toward me, and kiss him right there in the middle of the street.

When I pull away, Zach looks stunned and my cheeks feel like they're on fire, but I'm pretty pleased with myself. I kissed Zach! Time to bolt!

"Great seeing you!" I dart through the crowd before Zach can react, slipping through a line of people waiting for makeup tutorials. My heart is still pounding when I hear my phone ping. I click the phone on my ear.

Reese

I've got the charger. Where are you?

I scan the crowd for my sister, but I don't see her.

"Harper!" Reese yells. "Over here!"

My mouth falls open when I see her. Reese's eyes are lightly rimmed in a gray kohl liner with the palest tan and pink eyeshadow. There is a slight blush to her freckled cheeks, and she's wearing one of the new Barely There lip glosses. I almost wish I could take a photograph of her makeup to remember how to do it that well myself. Where did my baby sister go?

"You look so good!" I gush, stepping closer. "And so much like me at twelve and a half."

"Don't flatter yourself." Reese folds her arms across her Face of Beauty tee she slipped on when we arrived so that she could help run things.

Instead, she's basically eaten all the food and done all the activities, but that's fine. She's twelve and I'm twenty-two now, so I have to work. "Nice." I glare at her, and she glares back. "I change my mind. All I see is the fiery two-year-old who smushed my lipstick into my rug."

Reese rolls her eyes. "Are you still talking about that? You got a new rug right afterward anyway, so I did you a favor. Your room got a complete reno."

"Really?" I brighten. "I wish I remembered that."

"Well, maybe you can see it happen for yourself." She holds out my old phone in its battered case, and I feel the air leave my lungs. "I fully charged it, and it works. It's ready to go."

I stare at Reese's outstretched hand.

"I checked. The TikTok app is on it. I don't see the filter you were talking about, but it doesn't sound like anyone other than you has ever seen it anyway." Reese waves the phone at me again. "Hello! Aren't you going to take the phone?"

My mind is whirling, and my whole body is starting

to sweat, which means my makeup is going to melt off me like I'm in a horror movie. "I'm not sure." I look at my sister cautiously. "What if I get it to work and I mess things up again?"

Reese puts the phone in my hand. "You won't."

"How can you be sure?" I'm starting to get a chalky taste in my mouth again. All these thoughts are rumbling through my head. I can see Zach and Ava in the cafeteria laughing so hard milk comes out of Zach's nose, little Reese running with my phone in her hand, and Milo with his favorite squeaky shark toy, the Cambridge Street Girls walking together in a pack through the middle school halls, and a Blake video I used to like to dance to.

"I know you—well, *today's* you—and I like her." Reese hops on her toes. "I think you do too. So go back and be *that* person."

Suddenly, it feels like the whole world is spinning. I take the phone from Reese's hand and swipe through the apps on the familiar phone screen till I see TikTok appear. The app smiles up at me. I hesitate to open it. Do I try this right here? Or should I find a bathroom? There's an RV bathroom on-site with stalls behind me that I could step into. I look at the bathroom. Reese nods encouragingly. I take a step. Then I rush over to Reese again and hug her.

"I promise to be a better sister," I say, squeezing her so hard, I'm sure it hurts us both.

"You better be," she says. "Now let go of me. I have another puppy yoga session in five." She unwinds herself and walks back to the party without a care in the world. Which is how I want to be again.

I move toward the bathroom again, when I hear someone calling my name. What now? When I turn, I see Saya running my way.

"Did you hear the news?" she asks, sounding out of breath. "No, you've probably been too busy. Check Celia's social media."

"Ummm . . ." I may be a bit better equipped to make calls or take calls on these new super-tiny phones, but pulling up an app is out of my league. "My phone is dead," I lie.

Saya frowns. "Really? How? These phones have seven-day battery lives. I'll do it." Saya pulls up a screen using her own phone and opens an app. The first post I see is a handwritten note from someone named CeliaBeauty. Next to it is a glamour shot of Celia. I read fast.

Hi, my beauties! Oops on my part! Face of You announcement premature. You'll get something new from me soon enough, but it won't be this. I'm ever-evolving, my lovelies! More soon when I have news to share! xo C

Saya smiles triumphantly. "I spoke to my friend who works for Jameston, and apparently Blake called and threatened legal action if they go through with Celia's deal, citing copyright infringement, so now the deal is off. She's blown up her life on her own."

So have I, but Blake, being the class act she is, hasn't announced what I did yet. Guess those loose ends Celia said were "all tied up" weren't. "Karma," I say with a shrug.

"Karma," Saya repeats with a grin. "Hey, some of us are going out after the event to celebrate. You want to come?"

Saya is asking me to hang out? I didn't see that coming, but I can't say I dislike the idea. Away from Celia she's different. Maybe we all are. "Thanks. I'll catch up with you later." Saya nods, and I slip inside the floral-scented bathroom. It's empty, so I lock the door behind me.

To be safe, I head into a stall and lock that door too. I can still hear the party going outside and lots of barking, but I try to concentrate. My fingers are trembling as I pull out my phone and click on TikTok. I start to scroll through the feed like I did only hours ago, but it's hard to concentrate. In my head, I can hear Ava banging on the bathroom door at Sugar Crazy, the texts from Zach pinging like crazy, the fears I had about all the CSGs knowing I wasn't invited. I see other images too—me having breakfast with Blake at One Eighty-Five, driving with Reese, seeing Ava with her friends at their apartment, me kissing Zach.

I wish . . .

I keep scrolling. Ten years later, TikToks are pretty much the same—lots of dancing, cooking, babies and dogs, transformations, and green screens about super-hero movies.

I wish . . .

I click on new posts and look at the different effects options that are trending: portrait mode, color bursts, bling.

I wish . . .

My hands are shaking. What if the filter isn't on here? What if I made this up in my head? What if I never get to play with Milo again or sit down to dinner with my parents and Reese? Hang out with Ava and Zach or go to the prom? Is this it? Am I going to be stuck being twenty-two, never really having experienced life?

I wish . . .

I keep scrolling, feeling a ringing in my ears and that chalky taste in my mouth. My heart is beating so hard, I worry the whole world can hear it. The barking outside the bathroom has increased, and the sound of people laughing grows louder. I keep scrolling through filters, faster and faster now, and the thoughts come quickly.

I wish I could be twelve and a half again.

I wish I'd known Blake's life wasn't perfect. No one's is, and I should be happy with the one I got.

I wish I had the chance to experience everything—good, bad, even math class.

I wish I could go back and have a second chance with Ava and Zach.

I wish I never tried to be friends with Celia or the Cambridge Street Girls.

I wish I knew how great my life was already at twelve.

The birthday wish filter appears, sparkling and lighting up the screen! I'm so surprised, I hold the filter down as hard as my finger will let me press it. I take a selfie of myself and send my long-winded wish out into the world, blowing out the imaginary candles like I would on my birthday cake.

I wish! I wish! I wish!

The sounds outside the bathroom fade away, and the lights begin to flicker.

Then everything goes dark.

19

I blink twice as the lights flicker around me, then come on full blast.

It takes me a moment to get my bearings. I look around.

Bizarre black-and-white wallpaper with tiny silhouettes of people dancing stares back at me. I can hear the muffled sound of a fast-tempo song playing, and I'm standing in front of a toilet that has the words "SUGAR CRAZY" spray-painted on the lid.

"I'm back!" I scream, and kiss my phone. Then I dance around the small space, almost hitting my head on the pull-down changing station next to me.

"Harper? Please open the door. I just want to make sure you're okay."

Ava!

I reach for the door handle and pause.

I feel like I should look in a mirror first and just make sure I'm really, truly me again.

I spin around and grip the mirror above the sink.

My face breaks into a grin at the sight of twelve-and-a-half-year-old me with hair that doesn't quite curl and makeup that isn't anywhere near as perfect as it looked on Future Reese. I've got a pimple screaming to burst out on my chin, and the top I'm wearing isn't as cool as I thought it was a few hours earlier, but that's okay.

I'm me and I'm still trying to figure out who I am.

What I know for sure is that I no longer care about being a Cambridge Street Girl or trying to be someone I'm not.

I tuck my phone into my pocket and fling open the bathroom door, practically falling into Ava's arms. "AVA!" I cry, squeezing her so hard the three people online for the bathroom behind her look alarmed. "I missed you!"

"Um . . . we were only apart for five minutes, but okay," Ava says to my hair, which she's currently entangled in. "Are you all right?"

I slide out of the way so the next person can use

the bathroom. "I'm great! Like really great!" I can't help staring at her.

Future Ava looked exactly like Old Ava—or is it Current Ava? Regular Ava? It doesn't matter now. I'm back!

"I'm sorry for insisting we come to Celia's party," I blurt out. "You were right—she doesn't really want us here and who cares? I don't want to be here either." Ava's eyes widen. "The only thing I care about is being friends with you and Zach and getting my parents to agree to let me do that dog-walking business with you because I don't want you having roommates at Northeastern unless I'm one of them."

"Northeastern?" Ava's dark eyebrows shoot up. "As in university? We're twelve."

"We won't always be." I grab her hand. "Come on!" I rush through the loud, super-cramped dining room, where lit sparklers on giant ice cream concoctions are being served at tables and people are singing "Happy Birthday." But I don't need to sing. I already got my wish.

"Where are we going?" Ava asks as I drag her along.

"Home!" I say triumphantly. I rush into the glass-walled room where the Cambridge Street Girls are still poring over menus and their phones, occasionally looking up to take a selfie. I yank Ava over to Celia.

"Enjoy your party. Ava and I are leaving." Celia's mom is still on her phone in the corner, so I don't bother interrupting her.

"Cool." Celia sounds like she could care less. "See you tomorrow at my house to do a TikTok?"

"I don't think so." I smile.

This statement causes everyone to look up.

Celia's head pops up so fast, I'm sure it's going to fall off. "I'm sorry?" Heathers 1 and 2 look over worriedly.

"I said, if you want to make a TikTok that goes viral, you're going to have to do it on your own. You're not hitching a ride to my social media success or getting the chance to screw over Blake Riley. I don't even know if I want to work for Blake Riley! But I do know she's nice and she doesn't deserve her company being stolen by you. You're a terrible friend and an even worse coworker. And the last thing I want is to be a Cambridge Street Girl."

Celia's jaw drops, and she looks at the others at the table accusingly. "Did one of you ask her to be a CSG?"

"And you!" I stop in front of Saya. "Stop doing everything Celia tells you to do. You're better than that and actually kind of nice, and I think you should join science club. You like science! Who cares if Celia doesn't?" Saya's cheeks redden. "You deserve to be more than her intern."

"I'm not sure what that means," Saya says as she glances down at her menu, then up at me again curiously as I drag Ava out of the room.

"Harper?" Ava says, but she's laughing as I drag her past the hostess stand and out the door. "What just happened in there?"

I stand in front of the restaurant with its flashing lights and giant lollipop-shaped valet stand and try to catch my breath. "What happened is I decided we don't want to be friends with Celia Darrow or be a Cambridge Street Girl."

"Well, I already knew that," Ava starts to say.

"It took me a few hours, but I figured it out," I tell her. "We don't need Celia or the CSGs. We have each other and Zach." A tiny squeal escapes my lips as I think about our kiss again. "But I have a confession to make: I like him." I'm talking fast again. "And I think he maybe could sort of like me too, but neither of us wants to upset you. I still want to see what could happen but only if you'd be okay. So are you? Okay, I mean? Oh, and remind me to warn him not to eat any more Takis. They burn his tongue."

Ava is laughing harder now. "We can talk about the you-liking-Zach thing. And him-liking-you thing. It's not like I can't see it. I just don't want you guys messing up our group."

"We won't," I vow. "You guys will be friends forever, and he will help you with pet adoptions at the shelter someday."

"You're not making sense, but I like it." Ava stops laughing and points to a window. "Hey. Look. We're being watched."

I turn around. Celia and the rest of the Cambridge Street Girls are glaring at us. Or should I say all but one of them are glaring at us. Saya is smiling.

My work here is done.

"Let's call an Uber and get out of here." I look around for someone to ask where the Uber stand is.

"Uber? We aren't allowed to take an Uber alone. We're twelve." Ava pulls out her phone. "I'll text my mom."

"No, I'll text someone to come get us." I'm about to text my parents when I think of a better idea. I get a reply right away. "Okay, our ride will be here in ten minutes."

And it really is only ten minutes before my grandma

rolls up in her red convertible with the top down and waves to us. "Someone need a ride?"

I dive into the front seat to hug her. "Thank you! I promise to always take your call from now on."

"Um . . . deal?" Grandma says, looking mildly concerned. "So where are we off to?"

"Home." I've never wanted to see my family so badly.

"Something is different about you." Ava pushes her dark hair out of her eyes as the wind picks up as Grandma drives away. "What happened in the bathroom?"

"A lot." When I look at my phone, I realize we've only been gone an hour, but it feels like a year. Make that ten years. "Oh! While I'm thinking of it, could we review math this weekend? I need some help."

"You want to review math?" Ava asks incredulously. "You hate math."

"I know. That's why I need help! To get my grades up! I'm going to college" I say, and then I fire off a text to Zach. *(Warning: Don't use the birthday filters on TikTok!)* He replies right back.

Zach

That bad, huh?

> You have no idea. Hang tomorrow? You, me, Ava?

Zach

> As if I'd make plans with anyone else.

> Bring your math notes. I need help.

Zach

> Done!

I smile. I'm not sure when I'll tell Zach I like him, or when he'll tell me he has a crush on me, but we're going to figure it out. I'm going to figure everything out! I've only been Me again for fifteen minutes, but I already feel like I'm making progress. I guess I really can be efficient like Future Me when I want to be. When I think about it, planning the Fenway animal rescue event was fun. Maybe I have a future in party planning? Or public relations? Or marketing? I'm not sure, but the great thing is I have a lot of time to figure it out.

"Harper, I watched that Blake Riley video you sent me on TikTok," Grandma says. "She has spunk. I like her."

"Me too," I say, smiling softly as I pull up TikTok for a second and see Blake's latest post. She's dancing again, her hair looking as perfect as ever along with her makeup.

I make a small wish that Blake gets what she wants too. I guess I could DM her on here and tell her to make sure whatever she does in the future, she doesn't hire Celia, but something tells me Blake will be okay. I will be too.

As Grandma rolls up to the house, I see the lights on in the living room and my parents playing with Reese on the couch. She must have woken up, which is perfect. Just the sight of her pudgy little face has me bolting from the car. "Bye, Grandma! Thank you! Ava, come on!"

"What has gotten into her?" I hear Grandma say as I run to the front door, hit the keycode, and burst into the living room.

"Harper?" Mom says in surprise as I dive across the couch and hug her, then my dad, then scoop Reese up and swing her in the air.

Ava stands there watching me.

"Reese! You're a star!" I cry, laughing as I squeeze her little body, which smells like applesauce. "You saved me."

Reese blinks, her brown eyes wide as she breathes shallowly and looks at me. "I SEE IT?" she says, and I laugh, then pull my phone out of my pocket and give it to her.

"Careful," Dad says. "She may drop it."

I nuzzle Reese's nose as she pushes at my phone screen. "I think she knows what she's doing." I look at my parents. "And so do I. Mom? Dad? I know now isn't the best time because you're putting Reese to bed, but tomorrow I want to talk during Reese's nap. I'm going to give you my TED Talk on why Harper is old enough to go into business with Ava."

Mom smirks. "Your TED Talk, huh?"

"Yes, and I know what you're going to say—I'm too young, but I'm not. I'm ready for more responsibility. I'm not saying I want to be twenty-two overnight, but I can handle more. You just have to trust me."

Mom stands up and hugs me. "We do trust you. I guess I just worry. It's my job as a mom—to worry about you—but you're right. You're growing up, and we need to listen." She touches my chin. "Tomorrow during Reese's nap you can do all the talking."

"As a matter of fact, we did some talking while you were out." Dad looks at Mom. "And we're going to hire a sitter for Reese in the mornings so we can all get out the door quicker. And on weekend nights sometimes too. It's not fair to always make you watch her."

"I want to watch her," I insist as the three of us huddle together, the sound of Reese pushing things on my phone breaking the silence, "just not all the time." We laugh. "Oh, and can Ava stay for a bit since we left the party early?" I want to start working on our dog-walking flyers. I just know I can convince my parents to say yes.

Mom grins. "Sure." She goes to take Reese out of my arms. "I'll take this one so you guys can be alone."

I hold tight to Reese. "That's okay. She can stay." Mom looks at me strangely as I head up the stairs to my room and Ava follows. "I'll just let her play with some of my stuff till she gets tired." I turn to Reese and whisper in her ear, "I'll give you some lipsticks."

Reese whispers back, "LIP-STICKS."

"Good girl."

Hey, I've got to make sure that room reno Future Reese promised still happens. But other than that, I think I'm going to like being twelve and a half again. This time around, I feel a little bit older, a little bit wiser, and a whole lot of me.

Acknowledgments

●　●　●

"I love *13 Going on 30*." With that one fateful statement, my editor, Kelsey Horton, sent me off and running on a journey to create a story that is both a love letter to one of my favorite movies and something entirely new and relevant to the world today. Thank you, Kelsey, for being such a wonderful collaborator and an editor who offers guidance and serves as this book's fiercest cheerleader. I love working with you! Special thanks also goes to the rest of the Delacorte Press team, including Beverly Horowitz, Wendy Loggia, Tamar Schwartz, Lena Reilly, and Natalie Cavanagh, and to Suzanne Lee for the pitch-perfect book jacket design.

To Dan Mandel, thank you being my sounding board and guide through publishing, especially during the last two years.

To my beta readers and dear friends Mari Mancusi, Elizabeth Eulberg, and Lindsay Currie—even though we live hundreds of miles apart (and Lindsay and I have never met in person!), I have never felt so connected to you. Thank you for the invaluable advice and notes on this book. The same can be said about Kieran Viola, Soman Chainani, Sarah Mlynowski, Alyson Gerber, Tiffany Schmitt, and Julie Buxbaum. If the last two years have taught me anything, it's that the kidlit community is truly a family, and I feel thankful every day to be a part of it.

To my family—Mike, Tyler, and Dylan—thanks for putting up with me joining TikTok for this project and for being both my collaborators and videographers. (Special thanks to Dylan for the unboxing video of me in my bathrobe that went viral because he was sure no one would see it) I'm so thankful for your love and support—and your groans when one of my TikToks seems "cheesy."

And finally, thank you to Jennifer Garner and Taylor Swift—your movies and your music, which I've always loved, served as wonderful escapes for me during the pandemic, and were the perfect inspiration. This one is for both of you.